ROSEBUD HEARTS

JULIA CLEMENS

PICKLED PLUM PUBLISHING

For Cari, Amber, Jenny, and Allison. My girls.

CHAPTER ONE

CALLIE'S HEART raced as she put the final touches on her hair with fingers trembling from the adrenaline rushing through her body. The night had finally arrived: the grand opening of the Lodge. Their Lodge. She'd dreamed of this moment for months.

No, she'd dreamed of this moment for *years*, ever since as an eighteen-year-old girl she'd sat with her best friends, looking up at the historic lodge that personified their hometown of Rosebud. Half of the group had known they would be leaving town—some the very next week—but they had also somehow known that one day they'd come back to one another. And to the Lodge.

And now they were here. Finally, the insane renovations were over and the place was practically perfect in every way. The suites all had that rustic and homey, yet still luxurious, atmosphere expected by anyone visiting Rosebud. Crisp white tablecloths covered every table and little white-flowered centerpieces adorned them in the small but elegant attached restaurant. The restaurant menu was set, relationships with vendors had been established, and the first shipments of food had already arrived so that Saffron could cater the evening's event. The back offices where Callie and her friends would do most of their work were free of the cobwebs that had collected under the last owners. And best of all, the lobby and surrounding grounds were welcoming, well-trimmed, and beautifully outfitted.

"We did it," Kenzie exulted, joining Callie in the bathroom where she was getting ready. Their eyes met in the mirror, shining with excitement and nervousness.

"Don't jinx it," Laurel called from the main area of the suite.

The girls were getting ready in one of the Lodge's empty rooms. They had needed to be together as they prepared for one of the biggest nights of their lives. And for now, there were still a few empty suites because only their grand opening's out-of-town guests would be staying the night. But tomorrow that would all change. For weeks, Kenzie and Callie had poured themselves into their media campaign to fill those rooms. And they finally were. The very next night, each and every room would be filled. The Lodge was officially at capacity, and that felt amazing—especially considering how deep in the red they were, thanks to the extensive renovations. Kenzie had calculated that if they could stay at or near full for the first year of operation, they'd be in the black. Of course, that was almost unheard of for a new business, but with the experience each of the girls brought to the team, it made sense that their success would come quickly. They were all excellent at what they did.

The Lodge was coming into their lives at just the right time.

Kenzie scoffed in response to Laurel, but stopped boasting. None of them were very superstitious, but at the same time, why invite anything to go wrong?

The nervous tension in the room was palpable. They all knew tonight had to go off without a hitch. Otherwise, well, it wouldn't bode well for their future.

Hazel whistled as she squeezed into the bathroom with

Callie and Kenzie, making it feel small. The Lodge's suite bathrooms weren't tiny, but they weren't enormous, either. And three women getting ready for a glamorous evening took up a lot of space.

"Lookin' hot, Call," Hazel said as she leaned toward the mirror and fluffed her gorgeous blonde hair. Hazel had kept her locks long over the years. They were thick, luscious, and, much to the dismay of the many who were already jealous of Hazel, her color was all natural. She wore a knee-length black dress with about a million straps. On anyone else, it would have looked like spaghetti gone wrong, but on Hazel's toned and tanned shoulders, it was jaw-dropping. God had dealt Hazel a royal flush in the looks department.

Callie responded with a very unladylike grunt. She had tried to look pretty that evening. She wore a simpler, form-fitting black dress. It was off the shoulders, and although she didn't have Hazel's natural tan, she had to admit her pale shoulders looked relatively decent. Her shoulder-length blonde hair was thin but worked well with her slicked-back hairstyle. She knew she looked nice, and could have believed a good number of compliments, but being called hot when Hazel was in the same room? It just didn't work. Callie was acceptable, maybe even cute. But hot was out of her reach.

"You are," Kenzie agreed.

Like the others, their brunette friend wore a little black dress. Even though it was a joyous occasion, black was consistent and professional, and the girls wanted to put forward a united, competent front. So they wore black dresses all around, although each dress was tailored to the wearer's personality. Kenzie's fit her like a second skin, stopping at the middle of her calves. It had elegant capped sleeves, and when she turned around, it became showstopping. A daring triangular cutout showed off one of Kenzie's best features: her legs. Her dark hair was pulled back into a loose bun, a few tendrils artfully framing her face.

Laurel was likewise striking in her less formal A-line dress with thick straps and a skirt that fell just past her knee, and Saffron would turn heads with her effortlessly chic look: black pencil skirt and flowy blouse.

In short, Callie's friends were all beautiful, and she wasn't even in the same league.

"Nope, the four of you are gorgeous. I hit the scale somewhere between cute and pretty," Callie replied confidently. Being between cute and pretty was her ideal, the best she ever got.

Hazel stopped arranging her hair to stare at Callie. Kenzie narrowed her eyes, both hands going to her hips.

"That's not funny," she said sternly.

"I didn't mean to be . . . " Callie started, puzzled.

"You actually think that." Hazel sounded astonished.

"Yeah." Callie shrugged casually. Not everyone could be dazzlingly beautiful, and their group of friends was already uneven, with four of them almost too pretty for words. They needed something to offset them. Or rather, someone: Callie.

"You need glasses," Hazel said, shaking her head.

"Or better friends. How could we have allowed you to go through thirty years of friendship without knowing how incredibly stunning you are?" Kenzie asked.

Saffron pushed her way into the bathroom now, and Callie backed up against the sink to make room. The room was officially at capacity.

"Who doesn't know how stunning they are?" Saffron asked.

"Callie," Kenzie and Hazel said in unison. All three turned accusing looks on their friend.

"She thinks she fits 'somewhere on the scale between cute and pretty,'" Hazel added.

"There's nothing wrong with that," Callie said defiantly. She wanted to flail her arms to emphasize her point, but there was no room to do that without hitting someone. She managed to twist around until she was facing the mirror again, pretending to check her makeup.

"There isn't. If it's the truth. But Call, you are hot. Especially tonight," Saffron said as Laurel joined them, somehow wedging her body into the cramped room. Callie was practically in the sink now.

"Yeah, you are," Laurel agreed, even though she had to have missed most of the conversation.

"That's what I said," Hazel told Saffron, and the women somehow found space to high five.

"Leo would be a fool not to ask you out tonight," Kenzie added in a lower voice, holding Callie's gaze in the mirror.

Callie felt her heart flip and then flop. She'd be lying if she didn't admit that deep inside she was harboring that very hope. She and Leo had hit it off when she'd hired him as contractor for the Lodge remodel. They'd become fast friends, and Callie could have sworn there was more. But then she found out he'd just gotten out of a marriage, plus there was the whole part about her being his boss . . . and the whole thing had been rather messy. Until now. The remodel was done. This would be the last time she'd see Leo—unless he asked her out.

Callie let her thoughts drift to the man who resembled Jason Momoa. When he picked up a hammer, she thought he was even better looking than the movie star. On top of that, he was kind—he brought her favorite coffee multiple times a week. He was hardworking—he often stayed after hours to complete his daily work. And he was funny—Callie couldn't count the number of times he'd made her laugh until her stomach hurt. How could a man like that possibly want a woman like her?

He couldn't. So even as she wished Kenzie's prediction would come true, her rational side knew it wouldn't.

And yet she admitted to herself that she'd taken extra effort tonight. Hope was a silly thing and didn't often listen to reason.

"I wouldn't hold my breath," Callie said, trying to sound self-deprecating instead of pathetic. She wasn't sure she pulled it off.

"I would," Saffron said emphatically.

The others nodded, and Callie would have hugged them all if they weren't so dressed up and in such a small space. But a group hug in that bathroom would probably end with someone falling into the tub or worse.

"I love you guys, and I love that you are blind to my faults," Callie said, gathering up her makeup and placing it in her travel bag.

"One of us is blind, and it isn't the people you're accusing," Laurel began, but broke off at the sound of a phone vibrating against the counter.

Callie hadn't just heard the vibrating; she'd felt it as well. She pulled her own phone from her pocket as Kenzie picked up her phone from the countertop.

The five of them looked at one another, knowing if she and Kenzie were getting notifications at the same time, it had to do with reservations. They'd all cheered as reservation after reservation had come in during the past few weeks, but this felt different. Callie wasn't sure why they were all thinking this must be bad news. But judging by the looks on each and every one of their faces, they all felt that something was wrong.

"It's a cancellation," Kenzie said, biting her lip.

Callie studied the information on her phone. "They were supposed to be here for two weeks."

This time the sinking of her heart had nothing to do with Leo.

"Not a big deal. One cancellation. I'm sure we'll be able to fill it in no time," Saffron said.

Kenzie nodded and looked up from her phone. "Yeah, I'm sure we can. We've had other cancellations before, and there's a waiting list since we were completely full."

It was true. But something about the timing of this didn't feel great. Especially since these guests had planned to stay for two weeks, starting the very next day.

The girls had known they'd taken a chance when they chose to waive cancellation fees. Basically, people could cancel up until the moment of their reservation. For some of their media campaigns they'd even let people know that if they didn't show up at all, they wouldn't be charged. Maybe that's why this felt like such a bad omen. If people were already cancelling, what percentage of people wouldn't come at all?

Callie's and Kenzie's phones buzzed again.

"Another one?" Hazel asked.

Callie nodded.

"But this time it was just a three-day reservation," Saffron said, reading over Kenzie's shoulder.

"Yeah," Callie said, trying to sound as upbeat as her friend.

The fact that people were actually taking the time to cancel was a good sign. It meant people respected them enough to tell them in advance that they weren't coming. Maybe it was even more of a sign that people *would* show tomorrow?

Callie had to think positively or she would be in a gloomy mood all evening. And she couldn't do that. Not after Laurel had worked so hard planning the night.

"I'm going down to the backyard," Laurel said.

They'd worried that the lobby wouldn't be large enough to hold the numbers they were expecting. Thankfully the RSVPs for their event had been incredible. Nearly ninety percent of their guests had answered in the affirmative, and a number of the out-of-town guests were already present after checking in that morning. Mari and Tai, two of Laurel's kids, had taken those guests on a tour of Rosebud for the past couple of hours, giving Callie and her friends plenty of time to get ready. Ben, Laurel's oldest, was downstairs overseeing the final touches of the party, and Alex, Saffron's sous chef, was staying on top of the kitchen and all of the catering for the party. Between their family, friends, and employees who were busy cleaning rooms and setting up for the party, everything was covered. All was well.

Perhaps *too* well. Maybe that was why Callie was expecting something to go wrong.

"And I'm going to head to the kitchen," Saffron said, slipping out of the bathroom before Hazel could detain her.

"Alex has it covered," Hazel called after her.

"I just want to make sure," Saffron called back. Callie heard her open the main door to the suite.

"You'll just get in the way," Hazel said, but the only response was the sound of the door closing.

"She's going to get in the way," Hazel reiterated to Callie and Kenzie, since Saffron had ignored her.

"Preaching to the choir," Callie said as she took one last look in the mirror. It was as good as she was going to get.

"He'd be lucky to have you," Kenzie said, turning Callie by the shoulders so she had to look at her.

"You have to say that. You've been my best friend for thirty years," Callie replied, gazing at Kenzie's knees. She couldn't take the pity in her eyes.

"No, I'm saying that *because* I've been lucky enough to have you as a best friend for thirty years," Kenzie said. She gently squeezed Callie's shoulders and released her, taking a small step back. Kenzie knew Callie well enough to understand that this was too much emotion for her. Give Callie a headache-inducing problem that would make grown men cry, and she'd be fine. But hand her a bit of emotion and it made her want to run.

Callie endured Kenzie's heartfelt moment, and her heart actually felt a bit lighter, despite the cancellations and the fact that if Leo didn't ask her out tonight, it would be their final goodbye. Her breath started coming in short gasps. This was it. What if he didn't do anything? Although Callie had only known the man a few short months, she couldn't imagine her life without him.

"Maybe I should ask him out?" Callie asked uncertainly, finally letting her insecurities show on her face. She was sure she looked like a desperate, crazy woman, which was exactly how she felt.

"Maybe," Hazel began thoughtfully, but Kenzie shook her head.

"You know me," Kenzie said. "I'm all about female power and women going after what they want, but in this case, I'm saying no. He needs to ask you out. Call, you need to know that he wants you as badly as you want him, or you'll spend the entire time you date him second-guessing everything. I have no doubt in my mind that if you asked him out tonight, he'd say yes. I've watched him, and it's written all over his face. But I think you need him to come after you, to show how much he cares."

Callie nodded, loving that her friend knew what she needed even before Callie did. These girls really were the best. And that was why this venture had to work out . . . for them. The Lodge had to be successful, because too many good women had put their all into it.

A knock sounded at the door and the three women looked at one another. Saffron and Laurel wouldn't be knocking, since they each had a key to the room. But who else could it be?

Hazel and Kenzie shared a smile.

"What?" Callie asked suspiciously. Apparently the other two knew something she didn't.

"I need to go help Laurel," Kenzie said awkwardly, backing toward the bathroom door.

"And I need to make sure Alex and Saffron don't kill one another," Hazel added, almost tripping on Kenzie as she hastened after her.

Something was definitely up.

"Do either of you want to get the door?" Callie asked, since they seemed to know who was on the other side of it.

"Don't look so confused, Call. It doesn't go with your dress," Hazel teased with a grin.

"Then tell me what's going on!"

"We know it's none of us at the door," Kenzie began. "And who else knows the Lodge like the back of his hand and could have figured out exactly where we are? Who else would be looking for one of us before the event begins?"

Callie's hands immediately dampened with perspiration. They couldn't mean . . . no. There had to be others.

"What about Bryan?" she asked, wiping her hands on the nearest towel. Kenzie had said her estranged husband was offering an olive branch by coming this evening.

"He's going to be bringing my parents. He knows I want peace, and what's the last thing my mother's constant worrying will bring me before an event like this? Peace. If he cares about me, he'll keep them all downstairs until I arrive," Kenzie said.

"And Dylan?" Callie gave her last shot, mentioning the man Hazel was dating. Not seriously, because she had gotten divorced too recently to be serious about anyone, at least in her book.

"He has a client meeting that goes right up until six," Hazel said, pointing at the clock in the bathroom. It was only five-thirty.

The knock sounded again.

"Besides, none of them knows the Lodge like Leo does," Kenzie whispered before escaping the bathroom, Hazel right behind her.

Callie held her breath as she heard the door open.

"Hey, *Leo.*" Kenzie emphasized his name so heavily Callie was sure the entire Lodge could hear.

"We were just on our way out. If you're here to see us we can walk and talk," Hazel said, a little too sweetly. Callie could just imagine the smug grin on Hazel's face. She still hadn't quite forgiven Leo for not asking Callie out already. She thought he should have thrown caution to the wind and gone after what he wanted.

"I'm actually here to see Callie," Leo replied. His voice was quiet but assured, the voice that made Callie's knees tremble and her heartbeat triple.

She leaned against the rack of towels behind her. Leo was here. To see her.

She gripped a towel but quickly let it go when she realized she might just yank the whole rack down. That was the last thing the Lodge needed tonight.

"We thought so," Kenzie smirked.

Callie closed her eyes. This was how she was going to go. Dying of embarrassment as she waited for the guy she really liked to finally ask her out.

She heard a shuffling sound. Callie guessed that her friends had moved past Leo, letting him in. The door closed and there was silence for a moment.

Had they left?

Callie felt her heart thumping in her throat as she waited. Should she go out and greet him? As soon as he saw where she'd been, it would be obvious she'd heard the exchange by the door.

Or should she wait? Waiting seemed like the better option,

considering how weak her knees and thighs felt. But it was too awkward to just stand there and wait for him to find her. She needed to move.

Before she could take a step, Leo entered the bathroom, a soft smile on his face.

"You look beautiful," he breathed.

And for some reason, Callie believed him. Maybe it was the way he said it or the look in his eyes or the fact that her wonderful friends had all told her the same, but Callie finally felt it.

"Thank you," she said, trying to sound like a professional. She was a successful woman with nearly thirty years of experience and thriving businesses under her belt, not a giddy teenager with a crush.

She pushed herself off of the wall.

She'd done well for herself throughout her career, and yet for all of that, no one could say that Callie had had the same success in her personal life. Was that why she felt so shy now?

On top of that, she'd never fallen so hard and fast for anyone. She'd never cared so much about a man noticing her, or finally asking her out, as she cared right now for the man standing in front of her.

"I guess our professional relationship is over," Leo said as he looked around the bathroom he'd remodeled. Callie was doubly thankful she hadn't broken the towel rack.

"You did an excellent job," Callie replied without really having to think. It was a good thing too, since her mind just kept repeating, *Ask me out. Ask me out, please.*

"I don't know if this is crossing a line," Leo began.

Callie shook her head and then realized he hadn't even mentioned what line he was possibly crossing, so she stopped, forcing herself to wait for his next words.

"Oh, the hell with it." He ran his hand through his hair

before meeting Callie's gaze. "Would you want to go out sometime? I know it's unprofessional of me, considering we worked together and I'm hoping we can continue to work together, but it's been driving me insane. I've wanted to ask you out since you drove up to our first meeting. And now I'm just blathering." Leo stopped self-consciously.

Callie smile had grown so large over the course of Leo's speech that her cheeks began to ache.

"Is that a yes?" Leo asked, his eyes dropping to her lips.

"Oh, right. Yeah, of course it's a yes. Would anyone actually say no to you?" Callie asked. blushing as she replayed her words in her head. She needed to play it a little cool.

But Callie wasn't really a cool person. She was just being herself. And thankfully, Leo seemed to like who she was.

He chuckled. "I don't know what anyone else would say because I don't care about anyone else. The only yes I want is from you."

Callie's smile somehow stretched even wider.

"So I'll call you?" he asked.

Callie nodded; no words seemed right.

"Okay." Leo's smile nearly matched her own.

"Can I walk you down to your party?" he asked, extending an arm gallantly.

He was chivalrous too? Callie was going to melt. But not now. For now she wanted to enjoy the moment. She could melt later, on her own bathroom floor.

Callie looped her arm through Leo's and gazed up at him, not believing her luck. She was going to a party to celebrate her Lodge, escorted by a man she couldn't have even dreamed up.

It all felt too good to be true.

CHAPTER TWO

LAUREL SAT on the ground behind the check-in desk, her back against the filing cabinets beneath the counter and a package of red licorice beside her. She'd nearly emptied the whole package on her own.

The past five hours had been just short of a disaster. Scratch that, they'd been a full-fledged disaster.

Kenzie sat on a stool next to her, facing the lobby door with a fixed smile on her face as she waited for no one. Laurel knew no one was in the lobby because it had been practically empty since noon—check-in time. Only three of the eighteen parties they'd been expecting had come.

Laurel felt her eyes heating, a sure sign that tears were next, so she grabbed another red vine. Anything to keep from crying, even her if her stomach already ached. At least the pain would distract her from reality.

"You're going to be sick," Kenzie warned from her stool.

"I already am sick," Laurel admitted, even as she kept eating.

The night before had gone beautifully, giving every indication that the Lodge would be a roaring success. Everything had been in place—the food was delicious, the music tasteful and fun. The guests Mari and Tai had been showing around town had trickled down the stairs, many of them documenting the event with their cameras. They'd gushed about how gorgeous the Lodge and Rosebud were. They'd loved the food. They'd exclaimed over their rooms.

And then the local guests had shown up, every one of them complimenting what the girls had done for the town's landmark. Each of the Rosebud Girls had spent time interacting with these important guests, as well as with their loved ones who'd shown up to support them. Leo had stayed by Callie's side all night, and she hadn't stopped beaming. Kenzie and Bryan had made the rounds like any married couple, and Hazel had taken Dylan's arm, making the man light up like a birthday cake. Saffron had shown off the Lodge to her mom and siblings, and Laurel's her wonderful kids had spent the entire afternoon helping her, supporting her through the party as well. With their families, friends, and guests, they'd partied the night away. It couldn't have gone better.

"I still don't get it," Laurel said, leaning her head back and hitting it on a metal handle. She hardly even felt the pain. Had the sugar made her immune to pain? "We had the greatest of grand openings. We had the reservations. What happened?"

Kenzie shrugged, again attempting to smile. She was still holding out hope that their reservations were simply late, even though it was over five hours past the time guests should have arrived.

To keep costs down, they hadn't yet employed someone to be at the check-in desk around the clock. They'd figured that could wait until they got busier. They'd hired extra people for the party the night before and they had a few housekeepers, groundskeepers, and kitchen help on hand, but other than that, the girls were trying to manage it by themselves. That would be fairly easy if no one showed up . . . a bright side?

For some reason it didn't make Laurel feel any better.

"This is all my fault," she muttered around yet another red vine. She was truly going to be sick soon.

"If you say that one more time . . . " Kenzie admonished, but Laurel went right ahead. There was no point in tiptoeing around the truth.

"It's because of Bennie. He's still the number one hated man in town. And I was married to him when he committed his crimes. Guilty by association, or maybe even just guilty. I could have been a coconspirator without even knowing." Laurel slapped a red vine on her knee.

"First, I said don't. Second, what could any of this have to do with Bennie? None of these guests are from around here. And third, you can't have been a coconspirator without being aware of what he was doing," Kenzie said. Standing up, she kicked the bag of red vines away from Laurel.

Laurel crawled across the floor to retrieve them.

"Getaway drivers. They get prosecuted all the time. And they could have just been sitting there," Laurel argued as she settled back against the cabinets, her red vines back in her lap.

Kenzie drew her eyebrows together. "What are you even talking about? And when has that ever happened? Some innocent person who didn't know they were a getaway driver was prosecuted for being one?"

"All the time," Laurel claimed.

"That sugar is making you loopy."

"And this situation is making me mopey."

Laurel began to laugh at the near rhyme she'd made without meaning to.

Kenzie leaned over to swipe the bag of candy. "I'm cutting you off."

Laurel started to protest but realized it was probably a good idea.

"I'm guessing we can't stay in the black with only three rooms booked tonight?" she asked, even though she already knew the answer.

Kenzie blew air out of her nose, and Laurel took that as a *no*.

"But at least we had twenty rooms filled last night." Laurel was trying to find a brighter side now that her red vines were gone and she had nothing to keep her from crying.

"We comped all of those rooms since they were our guests," Kenzie said shortly. She dug into the bag of red vines and came out with two, tossing one down to Laurel.

"Has anyone else checked in?" Callie asked from somewhere above Laurel. Laurel didn't know where Callie had been, but wherever it was, she'd probably been working a lot harder than Laurel.

Kenzie shook her head.

"Pass me one of those," Callie demanded, and Kenzie handed her the bag of candy. At least Laurel had been of some help.

"This is my . . . " Laurel began again from her spot on the ground.

"If you say this is your fault one more time, I'm going to rain this candy over your head," Callie declared. "These reservations not showing up? They weren't local. No one cares about Bennie or your connection to him beyond Rosebud. This is bigger than you."

Laurel swallowed. Callie might be right . . . but that was almost worse than if all this were Bennie's fault. At least, if the missing reservations were connected to Laurel and Bennie, there might be a light at the end of the tunnel somewhere. If they had a reason for why things were going wrong, maybe they could come up with a solution. But if they couldn't blame Bennie, they had no idea why eighty percent of the reservations had either canceled or been no-shows. And no way to fix their problem.

"What are we going to do?" Kenzie asked.

"First off, we stop that stupid promotion. Guests need to pay a deposit when they make a reservation," Callie said.

Kenzie nodded.

Callie and Kenzie had brilliant business minds, but they'd never been in the hospitality business. It looked like waiving the deposit was biting them in the butt. At the time it had seemed worth the try, and now they knew it wouldn't work. They would all live and learn . . . at least, if they could get more business.

"How many new reservations do we have today?" Callie asked.

Kenzie logged into her computer and shook her head as she read the numbers she and Laurel had checked less than an hour before.

"None?" Callie asked.

Kenzie nodded, that one brief motion conveying her disappointment.

"Did you already stop the promo?" Callie asked hopefully.

If the promo was no longer going, that could explain why reservations had slowed.

"No," Kenzie said quietly, an uncharacteristic note of defeat in her voice.

"Something is going on. This doesn't make any sense. We were full, and nothing has changed since yesterday. And now we're getting nada?" Callie asked, beginning to pace.

Kenzie nodded again.

Laurel stood, feeling guilty that she was still moping on the ground while her friends were trying to work out a solution.

"I could quit," she offered, still suspecting that her past with Bennie might be a factor. She didn't know how it was all connected, but it was the only thing that made sense. None of the others had skeletons in their closets quite like Laurel's.

"No," Callie and Kenzie said in unison.

"We need you more than ever now," Callie assured her. She scrubbed a hand over her face.

Laurel hated that Callie was so stressed because of this. She had seen the way Callie and Leo had interacted the night before, and she knew they had already set another date—their official first date. Callie had liked Leo for so long. She should be celebrating that. And Kenzie: Bryan had shown up for her, something that wouldn't have happened a couple of months before. They'd worked hard to get here. But at the moment no one could talk about that or even feel joyful. The Lodge was failing. And even though they kept telling her it wasn't, Laurel knew this was somehow her fault. It was all too strange to be coincidence. They were all too good at what they did to fail this hard. Something more had to be at play, but Laurel couldn't put her finger on it.

The sound of footsteps coming down the stairs caused them all to look up, readying smiles for their guest.

But it was just Hazel.

"Wow. Don't hide your smiles all at once," Hazel said as she joined them.

"They weren't real anyway," Kenzie said.

Hazel sighed. "Still bad news."

"It keeps getting worse," Callie groaned.

Hazel cracked her neck, a sure sign she was thinking hard. Hopefully coming up with something that would help.

"Are you folks hungry?" Saffron asked. She walked out of the kitchen and leaned on the counter next to Callie. "We still have leftovers from last night, and now I have to figure out how to get rid of the ingredients we ordered for a full house this week."

"Another expense," Kenzie muttered.

"The Rosebud soup kitchen would be happy for any and all donations," Callie said quietly. She rubbed between her eyes, probably warding off a headache.

"What are we going to do?" Saffron voiced what they were all wondering.

"If we continue like this, what are we looking at?" Callie asked Kenzie the hard question.

"Six months?" Kenzie said before adding, "I could always put in more money."

"I could too," Hazel said but Callie shushed them.

"No. We have six months to turn this around. And we will." She looked at each of them.

Kenzie bit her lip, Hazel frowned, Saffron rested her chin in her hand, and Laurel probably looked the most downtrodden of all.

"We will," Callie declared again as she crossed her arms over her chest. Gone was worried Callie. She'd moved into battle mode.

"Saff. Get into town. Drum up some business for our restaurant. If we don't have guests eating, we can at least get some local dine-in customers," Callie began planning.

Saffron nodded, letting her hand drop.

"Hazel, use that star power. I know we wanted to wait to use your influence for a lull in sales, but the lull came more quickly than we thought it would. Get on your social media and start proclaiming to the world how amazing this place is. Talk to your ex, your friends, whoever. Basically, in the most loving way, exploit every relationship you have."

Hazel chuckled.

"Oh, and don't talk about the no-paying-until-you-show-up thing. We're shutting that down right now," Callie commanded.

Surprisingly, Hazel just nodded in response, as if she'd been waiting for orders. Hazel hated being told what to do.

Laurel blinked, but somehow it also seemed natural that they were all waiting for Callie to direct them.

"Kenz, you and I are going to dig deep. Figure out what we need to make. Project numbers and then work on a new media campaign. Hazel can help as soon as she's done with her shout-out."

Kenzie nodded too.

Callie looked to Laurel. "Your job is to dig. Start figuring out what is going on, without any of your silly this-is-my-fault ideas. We can't keep hemorrhaging reservations. We need to keep them once they're made. Figure out why we lost all our reservations today, and why new ones aren't coming in. Basically, none of what we're doing will matter unless you're successful."

No pressure. But Laurel knew Callie was right. And she knew she was the woman for the job, because she was the only one willing to believe this could all be her fault, no matter what her friends said. The other women would blind themselves to that possibility, and whoever did this task had to be willing to look at every alternative.

"We're going to make this work," Callie insisted, looking each of them in the eye. She didn't add what they were all feeling. They *had* to make this work. Laurel and Saffron had nothing to fall back on. The other women were also pouring themselves into this venture.

"And in the end, we'll be grateful for this setback," Callie added.

"But will we though?" Hazel asked skeptically, causing the group to laugh as their somberness vanished. Callie's hope was contagious, and even without an answer to their questions, the women felt some of their joy and camaraderie returning.

"Maybe not," Callie admitted with a slight smile. "But we

will all be stronger . . . and closer. The only alternative is to let this tear us apart, and I won't let that happen."

Laurel believed her. She wasn't going to let it happen either. Looking around at her best friends, she knew they all felt the same.

"If anyone needs help, reach out," Callie directed.

The women nodded.

"We've got this," Callie promised.

And Laurel knew Callie had to be right. Because there was no alternative.

CHAPTER THREE

HAZEL LOOKED DOWN at her offending side as she waited for the nurse to call her back to an exam room. She hadn't been to a gynecologist in way too long. At first, she had been preoccupied with her marriage falling apart and then with the move back to Rosebud. Actually, if she was being honest, she hadn't been to a doctor for far too long before that. Maybe when Sterling was five?

But all that was changing today. Hazel had felt the tiniest lump in her right breast.

She breathed in and out slowly, trying to calm her racing heart. It could be nothing. It was probably nothing. Hazel was under so much stress at the moment, and while she loved almost every minute of it—her kids, the Lodge, Dylan—it was a lot for one person. And the stress was messing with her.

She probably didn't even need to be here. Breasts had all kinds of lumps and bumps and tissue and stuff Hazel didn't know about. But it was better to be safe than sorry, so she'd come in to have it checked out and then catch up on all of the other gynecological stuff that she'd put off for the last several years.

Fun.

Hazel had thought about telling her friends about her appointment, but figured it would worry them unnecessarily. She was most likely fine, so why make a big deal about it when they were also stressed out with the Lodge business and personal lives? She hadn't told Dylan for the same reason. At the moment, though, she kind of wished she could text someone. She hadn't expected this feeling of loneliness as she waited to be seen, this desire to share her fears with someone and be reassured that she'd be fine. But the girls thought she was meeting with one of Sterling's teachers, and Dylan assumed she was at work.

Her heart rate was climbing again. She needed a distraction. Opening her Instagram, she saw that yet another friend had shared her post about the Lodge. It would have been great news if they could have kept more of these danged reservations. Their system was going nuts, with people reserving rooms and then often canceling days or even hours later. At least now they were getting a small cancellation fee each time, but it wasn't enough. Poor Kenzie and Callie were being overworked by the plethora of reservations, and Laurel still had no idea why the cancellations kept coming. Granted, she'd only been searching for a couple of days, but they needed answers fast if they were going to stay operational.

Hazel hated that the Lodge was suffering, although it was doing much better than a few days ago, thanks to hers and her friends' media shout-outs. Kenzie had been thrilled and told Hazel they could stay afloat a few more months, thanks to Hazel's followers. At least her marriage had been good for something.

"Hazel?" the nurse called out. Surprised that she hadn't called her full name the way most nurses did, Hazel looked up to see Betty Handler. They'd been on the cheerleading squad together back in high school. No wonder she'd been more familiar.

"Betty!" Hazel exclaimed, hugging her old friend. It had been years since they'd seen each other.

"I heard you were back in town, but I haven't seen you around," Betty said with a friendly smile, leading Hazel back into the heart of the office.

"I guess you're a little busy, considering you work and you have . . . five kids?" Hazel asked. She wasn't sure if Betty had four or five children.

Betty nodded. "But only three of them still live at home."

"Still a handful," Hazel said.

"Still a handful," Betty agreed with a laugh.

"Let's get your weight and vitals." Betty directed Hazel to a scale.

"Best part of any doctor's visit," Hazel muttered sarcastically.

Betty laughed again, adjusting the counterweight as Hazel stood on the scale.

"So other than the job and kids, what's going on with you?" Hazel asked as Betty jotted down numbers.

"Not much. I make pancakes every Saturday morning and volunteer at my church on Sundays," Betty said.

Hazel smiled. It was exactly what she would have expected from Betty, who had always been a rock. Some people were flighty and adventurous, and others were the steady rocks. Betty was the latter, and although both were good, Hazel craved more rocks at this time of life. Surprisingly, Dylan had become a rock as well. He had been more of the flighty and adventurous type back in high school, but he seemed to have gotten the itch for thrills out of his system, and now he wanted to be what the people in his life needed. He wanted to be what Hazel needed, if she would just let him.

She hadn't been able to bring herself to do that yet.

"How about you?" Betty asked, guiding Hazel to an examination room.

"Divorced, moved back home with two kids, bought the Lodge with my friends, had a kid decide he wanted to leave me, renovated the Lodge with my friends, started dating Dylan. I think we're caught up." Hazel kept her voice emotionless as she gave a quick rundown of her last couple of years of life. At least the bullet points the gossips around town loved sharing.

"That sounds . . . "

Hazel waited for Betty to pry, either into her divorce from her famous husband or into dating Rosebud's favorite reformed bad boy. She'd learned that many in town were even more curious about Dylan than her divorce.

"Busy," Betty finished. Her voice was kind but professional, with no trace of curiosity or judgment.

Hazel breathed out a sigh of relief. She should have known Betty would understand Hazel's need to keep things private. Even when Hazel had dated Dylan back in high school and the other cheerleaders had clamored for every detail of the relationship, especially after Hazel's heart had been broken, Betty had been the one to shoo the vultures away.

"You could say that again. But I'm thankful for where I am. I think," Hazel amended as she pointed to her problematic right breast. She really was sure it was nothing, or at least she kept telling herself that, but until she heard the doctor confirm it, she wouldn't be able to breathe completely easily.

"We'll get Dr. Maddox in here," Betty said as she looked around the examination room, probably to ensure all was to the doctor's standards.

"I've heard he's young," Hazel said. "It's weird being an age where doctors are younger than we are."

"Way younger," Betty said with raised eyebrows. "But he's

good. I've entrusted my own health to him because he really is the best I've seen. Miles better than Dr. Thurgood." Betty mentioned the OBGYN Hazel had seen in high school, whom Dr. Maddox had replaced.

"That's what I've heard. And that's why I'm here. He went to UCSF, right?" Hazel asked.

Betty nodded. "Graduated top of his class."

"Now I wonder if the man is too fancy to take care of my female issues," Hazel joked.

Betty chuckled. "He's surprisingly down to earth. You all set?"

Hazel nodded.

"Take everything off and put this over you," Betty said, handing Hazel a piece of paper that would be better suited for wrapping a gift than her body.

"I hate these things," Hazel said, eyeing the insulting excuse for a covering.

"You and me both," Betty said with a commiserating smile as she left the room, closing the door securely.

Hazel quickly undressed, getting colder by the minute, and covered herself as best she could with the large piece of paper before settling on the exam table.

She glanced around the white walls that held posters of reproductive parts, information on how often one should come to the doctor, and a bunch of Christmas cards from families, most with babies. Hazel guessed these were babies Dr. Maddox had delivered.

A knock sounded on the door before it opened slightly, enough for a voice to come in but little else.

"All set in there?" Dr. Maddox asked.

Hazel looked herself over and decided this was as good as it was going to get.

"Yup," she replied.

Dr. Maddox entered.

"Good to meet you, Hazel," he said with a comfortable smile. So far so good. "I hear you're friends with Betty."

Hazel nodded in response.

"Apparently good friends, since she may have mentioned that she'll have my head if I don't give you the best care." Dr. Maddox took a seat on a stool. "Although, what she'd do with my head, I have no idea. Even my wife isn't all too fond of this ugly mug," the doctor joked as he drew an imaginary circle around his face.

They both laughed. It was easy for him to joke about being ugly because clearly he wasn't. But Hazel appreciated that he was trying to put her at ease.

"Looks like you haven't been to a gynecologist in a few years. I'm glad you're here now," he said. Hazel was relieved he didn't blame her for not coming in earlier. She hated when doctors gave her a guilt trip. Looking up from the file of Hazel's paperwork, Dr. Maddox met her eyes. "Any concerns?"

"I thought I might have felt a lump in my right breast. But it probably isn't a big deal." Hazel was starting to feel silly now. The lump hadn't been anything extraordinary, and if she had a cancerous lump, wouldn't she be able to tell immediately? She kind of felt like the woman crying wolf.

"Probably not, but let's check it out, shall we?" Dr. Maddox asked as he began Hazel's breast examination.

Hazel was thankful that his hands weren't cold. So many doctors she'd visited over the years examined her with freezing hands, and it was all Hazel could do not to jump out of her skin at the cold touch.

He quickly examined her left breast and then came to her right. His fingers moved a little more slowly and then paused.

"Hm," he said quietly.

He'd found the lump. Hazel couldn't feel it physically, but her gut told her that was why he'd paused.

"It's small," he said.

Hazel nodded.

Dr. Maddox ended the exam and sat back on his stool, meeting her eyes again.

"You do have a lump," he said matter-of-factly, in a way that made Hazel feel calm even though it was obvious he didn't think it was nothing.

"I'd like to get it checked out a bit more. Let's get you in for an ultrasound tomorrow."

Hazel's calm fled. An ultrasound? That sounded more serious than what should be recommended for a lump that was nothing. It had to be nothing, right?

"An ultrasound?" Her voice caught.

"It sounds a lot scarier than it actually is. You have two kids, right?" Dr. Maddox asked.

Hazel nodded, feeling her face going paler by the second. She needed water or air or maybe both.

"It's the same basic concept as pregnancy ultrasounds," he said.

Yeah, but when she'd had ultrasounds with her kids, they were looking at a baby. Now they were looking for . . .

"This is a precaution we take for any kind of lump," Dr. Maddox tried to reassure her, but Hazel was already heading down a spiral of panic and worry.

"Let's finish up your exam and then get you scheduled," he continued.

Right . . . exam. There was still more.

Hazel's panic ebbed and flowed as Dr. Maddox conducted the examination. Soon it was over, but Hazel wasn't sure what she felt. Did she have cancer?

Just the word was like an icy shock to her system. It was the kind of thing that happened to others, not to her. And yet here she was.

"I'm seeing the emotion all over your face. I know it sounds scary, but I can assure you that we conduct ultrasounds on all kinds of lumps and a good number of them end up being nothing. But I want to be sure, for both our sakes," Dr. Maddox said.

Hazel began to breathe again. She realized she'd been holding it the whole time the doctor spoke. But his words were comforting. She still wasn't thrilled at the prospect of coming back in for an ultrasound, but it was beginning to sound less terrifying.

"Do you have any other questions, concerns, anything?" Dr. Maddox asked as he stood.

Hazel shook her head.

"I'll have Betty come back in after you're dressed to set up the appointment for tomorrow," Dr. Maddox said, his voice steady. Exactly what Hazel needed.

Hazel nodded as he walked out. She wished it was already tomorrow. She wanted the ultrasound done and over.

She sat there for a few more moments before the cold demanded she get up and get dressed. A few seconds after she'd finished, a knock sounded on the door.

"Hazel?" Betty said.

"Come in," Hazel responded, rubbing her arms with a shiver. She'd worn a short-sleeved shirt and was now regretting that choice. She was so cold.

Betty took one look at Hazel before wrapping an arm around her. "I'm doing this as Betty your friend, not Betty the nurse," she clarified.

Hazel almost laughed. But the icy coldness consuming her wouldn't let her.

"Dr. Maddox told me we're going to be seeing you again tomorrow," Betty said.

Hazel nodded.

"I know it's scary, Hazel. I've been there," Betty said.

Hazel pulled away to look at her friend. What?

"I found a lump a couple of years back. I had this same appointment. I had to meet with an ultrasound tech the next day."

I know how it feels, Betty was telling her, and Hazel had never felt more glad for another's life experiences.

"What happened?" Hazel asked, feeling bad about prying but not bad enough to keep from asking her questions.

"What they found in the ultrasound was worrying enough for me to get a diagnostic mammogram. They didn't like what they saw there either, and I went in for an MRI."

Hazel shook her head, just imagining that scenario and how it must have felt.

"Finally, they did a biopsy and were able to confirm that the lump was benign."

At the happy ending to Betty's story, Hazel felt some hope.

"Really?" she asked.

Betty nodded. "Those were some of the scariest days of my life. I stayed up all night worrying for several nights in a row. I had to take time off work; I was a mess. So was Brandon," Betty mentioned her husband of thirty years.

"I can imagine," Hazel began but then realized she didn't have to imagine. She was living it right now.

"So can I give you a bit of advice, again as friend Betty, not nurse Betty?"

Hazel nodded. She would take any and all advice right now.

"Go out tonight. I know you're going to want to go home and curl up in a blanket and try to shut out the world, but I did that and it was such a mistake. It gave my thoughts way too much room."

Hazel could see how that could be a bad decision. Her

thoughts were already running rampant, and she hadn't even given them free rein yet.

"Have that handsome boyfriend take you out for a night on the town. Dance until your legs are about to fall off and you need to crash into bed so exhausted you couldn't think if you wanted to."

Hazel liked the sound of that. She hadn't danced in years, at least not the way Betty was suggesting.

"Tomorrow will come, one way or another. No amount of worrying or thought will keep it away. So embrace it. Enjoy tonight. Remember my story and live. You'll never regret that."

Hazel grinned at her friend, some of the coldness finally abating. Betty was right.

"Do they still do country swing night at Hellions?" Hazel referred to Rosebud's favorite country bar. She hadn't been there since high school, when she'd had to flirt with the bouncer to let her underage butt in.

"They do," Betty affirmed with a grin.

"Awesome," Hazel said, thankful to have a plan for the night. If she could just get through this night, the ultrasound would happen, and hopefully, that would be the end of all of this. Even if it wasn't, Betty was right—sitting around waiting for the morning would help nothing and no one. Tonight, Hazel wanted to live.

LOUD MUSIC PUMPED through Hazel's veins as Dylan twirled her on the dance floor. She laughed as she spun, first away from him and then right into his solid chest.

"You're good at this!" Hazel yelled over the music.

She had thought she was going to have to beg and barter with Dylan to get him to take her to Hellions, but he'd jumped at the idea. Seeing his skill on the country dance floor, Hazel began to wonder if he hadn't been here before.

"So are you," Dylan replied in her ear. He spun her out and then put both hands on her waist as they began to sway to the music.

The Hellions dance floor held the perfect mix of dancers performing fancy tricks like the one Dylan had just done with her and couples who just wanted to hold each other close to their favorite country ballads. The bar consisted of a few scattered high-top tables and a long counter along the back wall of the room. Most of the room was devoted to the dance floor that was filled to capacity, even though it was ten P.M. on a Wednesday night.

"Yeah, because I came here often in high school and then I married a country music singer. We went to this kind of place all the time before he made it big. What's your excuse?" Hazel narrowed her eyes playfully as she waited for Dylan's answer.

They both understood that the other had lived a full life in their time apart, and they were content with their differences as they slowly got to know one another again. Hazel in particular was still insistent that things between them stay relaxed, chill. She had yet to call Dylan her boyfriend, though she no longer corrected other people when they did. But in Hazel's mind, they were good friends who dated and really enjoyed kissing each other.

Dylan suddenly let go of her waist and took her hand, leading her off the dance floor. *Where were they going?*

When they got to a quieter corner of the bar, Dylan turned to face her and took both of her hands.

"Are we doing this now?" he asked.

"Doing what?"

"Talking about our pasts? Delving deeper?" Dylan's eyes were full of hope.

Hazel dropped his hands and took a sudden step back. Now was not the time for Dylan to think she wanted more from this. From him. She had yet to tell him about the lump. And what if she got bad news tomorrow and went through what Betty had, but didn't hear the word *benign*? She couldn't let Dylan into her life only to make him endure that, her problems taking over their relationship. It wasn't fair.

"I was just asking about your mad skills on the dance floor," Hazel said lightly and turned to go to the bar. She needed something cold. While she had been frozen at the doctor's office, now she was hot all over.

"Hazel," Dylan said as he spun her so that she was once again looking at him. "Just in case you misunderstood, I want to go deeper. I want this to be more."

Chills ran up Hazel's arms. She no longer needed that drink —she needed to get out of here. Things were closing in, and it was too much.

"Um," Hazel said as she put a hand to her forehead.

"But you're still just wanting to have fun?" Dylan asked, the disappointment in his voice louder in her head than the music could ever be.

"I thought you understood that," Hazel said, her breath coming too rapidly. Her life already had so much else going on. She didn't have the emotional bandwidth to deal with this too.

"I did. I mean, I do. I just hoped that after a while . . . "

"You'd wear me down and I'd become the woman you wanted all along. What? You were just biding your time dealing with who I am now, hoping that one day I'd be the woman you want?"

That wasn't what Dylan had said, and Hazel knew it. But now that she had let the words out, they felt good. That was what he was doing, wasn't he?

"Hazel, I didn't say . . . "

"You didn't have to say it, Dylan. I can feel it. You hate that I'm pushing you away, and you want me to be different. You want me to let you in."

"I do hate that you push me away, but I would never want to change you," Dylan said, trying to take Hazel in his arms.

But she stepped back again, away from his warmth. "Except that you do. If I do let you in all the way, it will mean I have changed," Hazel reasoned, bristling in annoyance. So much for a lighthearted evening to distract her from serious subjects. This was turning into something worse than sitting at home and worrying about tomorrow.

"I guess that's true, but we all change. Especially our wants. I know that your divorce . . . "

"Don't make it seem like I'm too broken to love you!" Hazel shouted, appreciative that the loud music was covering their heated conversation.

"Hazel, I would never say that."

"So I'm imagining all this?"

"Stop putting words in my mouth," Dylan said firmly, squaring his broad shoulders.

Hazel stood tall. She'd promised herself she'd never let a man direct or guide her again. She'd done that for too much of her life. So if that was what Dylan wanted—

She spun and started for the door.

She could hear Dylan matching her step for step, so she increased her pace. She didn't want to be near him. Even though her heart was beginning to ache, this was probably all for the best. She and Dylan had had a fun run, but it was time to get serious about the important things in her life. Like her kids and the Lodge. And, heaven forbid, if the worst happened with her health, well, she didn't need a man who was pressing to be more in her life.

"I drove you," Dylan reminded her once he and Hazel arrived in the parking lot.

"I can walk," Hazel said stiffly, looking down the gravel drive toward the main road that would take her home. After five miles, true, but even though she'd just danced for a few hours, her legs could still go a couple of miles.

"Not at this time of night, you won't," Dylan said. He lengthened his stride, passing Hazel and stepping in front of her.

"Who are you to say what I can and can't do?"

"Evidently not much more than a concerned citizen. You've proven you don't want me to be more," Dylan said quietly. He straightened, looking all too resolved. "But I wouldn't let any woman walk down a road like this at eleven P.M., much less the woman I love."

Hazel swallowed down the gasp that threatened to escape. Had he said *love*?

She felt her eyes begin to sting, but she wasn't going to cry. Not now. She felt guilty that Dylan had fallen in love with her, but she'd been nothing but honest from the start. He knew what this was for her. And if he'd fallen in love with her, well, that was on him.

"Whatever," Hazel said brusquely, the word hurting her as much as it had to have hurt Dylan. She didn't want to brush his feelings aside, but it was better for him this way. Even if she wasn't sick, she was too much of a liability. If he stayed with her, Dylan would eventually learn that loving her led to grief, not happiness.

"Just give me a ride home," she said, stomping to his truck.

Dylan stayed silent as he came to her door and opened it for her before getting into the driver's seat.

He was silent as he backed out of his space and left the parking lot for the main road. He stayed silent through the many turns that led them back to Hazel's house and even as he stopped in her driveway.

"Thanks for the ride," Hazel said, needing to break the damned silence before it broke her and made her say things she knew she shouldn't. Like the fact that she might not be in love with Dylan yet, but she could be. Or that she wanted to get deeper too, but now wasn't the right time. That she'd gone to the doctor and she might have . . . that last word propelled her out of her seat and out of the truck.

She waited for Dylan to say something, anything, but silence continued to reign, so she slammed the door shut behind her.

Fine. If he didn't want to say goodbye, she was fine. She'd be fine. She had her boys and her friends and family. She had plenty of people; she didn't need Dylan.

This was better for everyone.

And with that lie, Hazel walked up to her bedroom and promptly fell into bed, tears streaming down her face.

Betty had been right about one thing. A night out with Dylan had kept her from worrying about the next day. Now Hazel's thoughts wouldn't stray from the man she'd just pushed away. An incredible man.

He deserved so much more than she could give.

CHAPTER FOUR

"I'M TRYING to remember why I ever stopped eating these things," Kenzie said with an enraptured sigh as she wrapped her mouth around the gigantic burger Saffron had prepared for her.

The Lodge was nowhere near as busy as they'd hoped it would be at this point, but thanks to Hazel's work on social media, as well as the new ad campaign she and Callie had begun, things had picked up. A bit.

They were still at only a little over fifty percent capacity thanks to all of the cancellations, and Saffron's restaurant often had empty tables, but some beds were filled and the restaurant had been full the evening before at seven P.M. So there were silver linings. Kenzie just had to strain a bit to see them.

"Because you kind of had a stick up your butt?" Saffron said, joining Kenzie at the counter in the kitchen. Kenzie had cleared it off to enjoy her meal with Saffron. She was now second-guessing that decision.

"I did not," Kenzie declared, stuffing another bite into her mouth. She might be annoyed with Saffron's description, but she wasn't about to waste time talking, not when she could be using that time to stuff her face with the blue mushroom burger

Saffron had just added to her menu. Grilled bacon and onion jam and sautéed baby portabellas over a blue-cheese-stuffed burger was perfection in Kenzie's book.

"If you'd cut burgers from your diet because of your love of animals or for health reasons, I could have forgiven you. But, girl, you know you had a filet mignon at least once a week. It was all about your image. The woman you wanted to be didn't eat burgers. She was too stuck up for them," Saffron said with a smile that eased the accusation.

Kenzie knew she'd been a bit uptight before, but she wasn't this woman Saffron was describing anymore. Was she?

Her thoughts were cut off as Saffron strutted across the kitchen, back straight, kind of looking like she *did* have a stick up her bottom.

"That was you," Saffron stated as she stopped.

Kenzie gasped. "It was not."

She looked around the kitchen for someone to back her up, but only Alex, Saffron's friend, was paying attention to them. And Kenzie knew for a fact Alex would take Saffron's side. Although Saffron had yet to see the feelings Alex had for her, everyone else at the Lodge was fully aware.

"Just add a severe bun and a power suit and it was totally you, girl. But I loved you through it all and only say this now because you are so far from that woman you once were," Saffron returned to the counter and put a hand on top of Kenzie's.

Kenzie pursed her lips as she considered Saffron's words.

"You've relaxed since you moved home and quit that terrible job," Saffron continued approvingly, pulling her hand away and washing up before she began rolling out dough for her special that evening.

"I'm sure Bryan would concur with your assessment." Kenzie thought about all of the grievances Bryan had been brought up during therapy. Each and every one was along the lines of what

Saffron was saying. And the time at the therapist's had helped Kenzie to see that she'd created a false persona and worked to maintain it, sometimes at the cost of others. "But was I really that awful?" Kenzie wasn't exactly hurting from what Saffron had said, but she was curious.

She turned her attention to the fries beside her burger. Just in case Saffron's next words did sting, these would be her healing balm. The sweet potato accompaniments to her burger were nearly as good as the burger itself.

"Not awful. But definitely not the Kenz we know and love. Not the woman Bryan married. Not the woman I see in front of me today," Saffron finished softly, as if she were worried she was overstepping.

But Kenzie had asked the question. And the answer was surprisingly comforting. Saffron had just told her she was no longer that cold city woman. She could feel it too. Parts of her she'd repressed for so long, as they didn't fit her idea of a woman in the corporate world, were coming alive again.

"Bryan would definitely agree. But I think we're on our way back to something good," Kenzie said thoughtfully, popping another fry into her mouth. Maybe they were even on their way to something great. She and Bryan were both working hard to recover the marriage they'd almost lost. Although life wasn't easy or breezy, for the first time in years Kenzie was beginning to be proud of the wife she was trying to be. That was much more important to her than any kind of image.

"So things are going well with Bry?" Saffron asked, her eyes still on the dough.

She knew Kenzie would be more comfortable answering that question if the situation was as nonthreatening as possible. Avoiding eye contact helped her relax. Only someone as close to her as Saffron would realize that.

Thankfully, she had good news to relay.

"Things are getting better," Kenzie said between fries. "He's still living in the city, but he agreed with the therapist that we need to start dating one another again. So I have a hot date with my maybe-soon-to-be ex-husband next Friday," Kenzie joked.

Saffron looked up, horrified. Apparently Kenzie's joke had fallen a little flat.

"It was a joke," Kenzie assured.

"Don't joke about Bryan being your ex-husband," Saffron said, shaking her head. "You never know what just admitting that could possibly do to your psyche." She was right as usual.

The woman may have never been married, but she understood relationships much better than most. Or at least better than Kenzie did.

"But a date is great news," Saffron encouraged, deciding she'd scolded Kenzie sufficiently.

"Yeah, I kind of have butterflies thinking about it," Kenzie admitted, hiding behind her burger. She could feel her cheeks getting red.

"Aw, that's so cute," Saffron gushed.

It really was. Not that Kenzie would ever admit that out loud.

Kenzie's phone chimed and she groaned at the interruption. But she'd been able to finish most of her burger and fries, the closest thing to a full meal she'd had since the grand opening, so she should be grateful.

She wiped her hands on a napkin and pulled her phone from her pocket.

"Raquel?" Kenzie said aloud, frowning as she read the name of the person who'd just texted her.

"Your sister?" Saffron asked, raising an eyebrow.

Kenzie nodded, hating that she had a pit in her stomach. But hearing from Raquel typically meant one of two things: she needed money or she wanted Kenzie to relay bad news to their parents. She claimed that Kenzie was the golden child and their parents would never be mad as long as Kenzie delivered the news. Kenzie countered that of course their parents didn't get mad at her because the bad news wasn't her fault. Usually, Raquel had already hung up by that point, knowing Kenzie would do her bidding.

Kenzie was never a pushover—unless it came to Raquel. Her big sister had always been able to manipulate her, and as much as Kenzie hated it, she would have hated losing the relationship even more, so she continued to let Raquel exploit her.

"What does she want this time?" Saffron asked, raising a knowing eyebrow.

Kenzie had yet to read the text. She wasn't sure she wanted to. But she had to at some point, so she might as well do it while she had Saffron's support. Taking a deep breath, she tapped the phone screen.

"She heard I moved home but Bry is still in the city," Kenzie explained and kept reading. "And she wants to move home, too."

Kenzie gulped and set down her phone.

"With me."

Saffron's eyes went wide.

Kenzie's head began to ache. But this was good news, right? She'd always wanted a closer relationship with the sister who'd moved away when Kenzie was twelve.

"She says she'll pay me rent and that she misses me," Kenzie finished.

Saffron began shaking her head.

"What?" Kenzie asked, even though her common sense was agreeing with Saffron.

"It's not a good idea."

"It's not a terrible idea," Kenzie countered.

"I beg to differ."

Because Saffron had known Kenzie since kindergarten,

she'd had seven years in school with Raquel as well. To say Raquel wasn't the most capable big sister was like calling a hungry lion kind of temperamental.

"She's grown up," Kenzie defended.

"I'm sure she has. Enough that you want to live with her? When we're dealing with all of this with the Lodge and you're still trying to work through things with Bryan?"

"But what better time will there be? God willing, Bryan and I will get back together and then it would be awkward for Raquel to live with me, but this might be the exact right time. Besides, I don't think she'd be asking unless she was desperate," Kenzie finished.

"Do you hear yourself, Kenz? Your sister has to be desperate to live with you? And how did she get herself in such a desperate situation? I doubt that means she's a dreamboat to live with."

"She's my sister."

"Why not have her move in with your parents?"

"I can't do that to them."

"Yet you'd do it to yourself? Raquel could find her own place. I'd even help her find an apartment. But why go from seeing one another twice a year, at most, to living together?" Saffron nearly pleaded.

Kenzie understood. Part of her felt the same way. But in the end, only one thing mattered.

"She's my sister," Kenzie stated again.

———

KENZIE WAS SUPPOSED to have been at work an hour ago and yet she still stood in her driveway, waiting for Raquel to show up.

Against all of Kenzie's friends' advice, Raquel was moving

in. On a temporary basis—even Raquel agreed that was for the best. They'd made a month-to-month agreement, starting today. If Raquel ever showed.

Her friends knew Raquel wasn't a bad person. She just didn't notice things beyond herself. People thrived around her, as long as they stayed in her bubble. But invariably she'd move, leaving them floundering. And Raquel never seemed to care, at least not enough to behave any differently.

Where Kenzie had been power suits and severe buns, Raquel was flowy skirts and long, untamed hair. Where Kenzie was rigid and unmoving in her strict cleaning preferences, Raquel liked to allow her surroundings to tell her how they wanted to be treated. Kenzie needed order; Raquel needed freedom. Kenzie craved security, and Raquel craved adventure.

But surely they could live together for a month.

Kenzie brought out her phone to look at the time just as it dinged with a text. Her heart ramped up, but it was just Callie. *I know why you're late. No pressure. See you when we see you.*

If her friends had been wary of the two sisters living together, her parents had been downright against it. They'd insisted that Kenzie tell Raquel if she wanted to move back home, she could move in with them, but Kenzie couldn't do that. She was glad she'd talked her mom out of being there that morning. She could just imagine the *I told you so* look that her mom would be giving her as they waited for Raquel to show. If she showed at all.

Everyone had said it was too soon, that Kenzie should take more time to think about whether this was what she really wanted. Raquel had texted Kenzie on Tuesday, and it was only Thursday now, but Raquel had needed a place immediately and Kenzie wasn't going to change her mind, so why not start immediately?

A car turned onto Kenzie's street. Judging by the way it puttered along, barely holding together, a black plume of smoke following it, Raquel was here. Only an hour after the time they'd agreed to meet. Not a big deal.

Raquel pulled into Kenzie's driveway and parked, straddling the middle. Kenzie realized she'd have to ask Raquel to move so that she could pull her car out of the garage to go to work, but that wasn't a big deal either.

Raquel pushed open her car door and raced toward Kenzie, enveloping her in a hug so tight Kenzie forgot all of her trepidation. This was her sister. Her only sibling. She could make some sacrifices.

Kenzie felt some of Raquel's hair in her mouth as she opened it to greet her sister.

Pushing it out of the way, she said, "I'm so glad you're here, Racky." She hadn't used the childhood nickname in years. When Kenzie was little, she couldn't say Raquel, so she'd come up with Racky, and the name had stuck. At least until Racky had moved out.

"I'm so glad to be—" Raquel started to reply, but her voice was swallowed up by the sounds of barking.

Raquel pushed away from Kenzie and returned to her car, opening the back door and letting out three dogs that somewhat resembled bears.

How did they all fit back there? was Kenzie's first thought. Her second was, *Oh my gosh, Raquel plans on having those horses live with us.*

Kenzie had never been an animal person. She didn't hate them; she actually appreciated them when they were at a distance or at someone else's home. But in her own?

And who would take care of them? Kenzie worked long hours at the Lodge, and Raquel had promised to find a job as soon as she arrived. These dogs looked like the type to need a lot of feeding and attention.

"Bryan's allergic." Kenzie stated the most important reason she couldn't have pets, especially furry dogs.

"But he doesn't live here, silly," Raquel said, cuddling two of the dogs. The last dog looked up at Raquel, his big eyes causing even Kenzie to melt, but Raquel ignored it and turned to her sister. Raquel didn't mean to be cruel, but sometimes she became so self-absorbed that she didn't even realize that she was neglecting someone, even the sweet dog she loved.

"But I'm hoping he will live here soon," Kenzie reminded her.

"And the dogs will be gone when I am."

"But the fur . . . "

"You worry too much, sissy. It'll all be fine," Raquel said, pulling Kenzie into a side hug.

"Can we at least keep them outside? The weather is nice and . . . "

"No can do, Kenz," Raquel said cheerfully, breezing past Kenzie and leading her little menagerie toward the house. "They're indoor dogs through and through. But don't worry. You'll never notice them."

Kenzie eyed the gorgeous but huge dogs. That didn't seem likely.

But again, this wasn't a big deal, right? Her sister was here. Living with her. And Kenzie was only going to be a little over an hour late for work.

Raquel was right. It would all work out.

CHAPTER FIVE

HAZEL EYED the coffee mug in front of her, noticing that it looked a little blurry around the edges. Her poor body was so tired she couldn't even focus on the most mundane of tasks.

But somehow she'd managed the important stuff. She'd gotten Sterling off to school, driven to work, and now she was in her office, trying to help Kenzie and Callie with their ad campaigns. Unfortunately, her brain didn't seem to want to cooperate. She took a gulp of the creamy coffee, willing the caffeine to reach her brain.

Better. But still not great.

Hazel hadn't slept well in nearly two weeks. Ever since she'd broken up with Dylan. Assuming one could really call that a breakup when they hadn't ever truly been together. But it was better that she'd pushed him away, especially considering the past two weeks.

She'd spent what felt like every day since then at some doctor's office or hospital, lying to everyone about where she was going. She wasn't ready to tell her friends anything yet. She wanted good news before she scared them with what she was enduring. So she'd gone to her ultrasound appointment and then the diagnostic mammogram. The MRI had been . . . fun. Hazel had never wondered what it would be like to be buried alive, but if she had, she was pretty sure it would mirror her MRI experience. She'd never been claustrophobic, but that chamber put her close. And then the lovely biopsy. That needle going right into her breast? She shuddered just remembering it. Thankfully, she'd been given a local anesthetic, but Hazel had never been fond of needles and that one would live in her nightmares for a while.

But she'd done it. She'd endured every last test, and now here she was. Ready to get the call from her doctor telling her all was well, that all of her worrying was for naught. Even though she'd tried not to worry about what was going on in her body, even though most of her thoughts swayed toward Dylan and whether she'd made the right decision with him, there was always that niggling doubt in the back of her mind that maybe she was wrong. Maybe this lump really was something.

Like cancer.

But Betty had been right. There was no point in borrowing problems from the future. If she had cancer, it was a future problem. A very near future problem, but she couldn't do anything about it yet, so worrying was useless.

Sterling had been the hardest to keep in the dark, but also the last person Hazel could tell about her doctor visits. Her sweet boy had always been empathetic—maybe too empathetic —and the stress of this would be too much. If Chase was around, maybe things would be different, but Hazel would not allow her youngest son to carry that kind of burden all by himself.

"Are things getting settled with your attorney?" Callie asked as she came into Hazel's office and took the empty chair across from her.

That had been Hazel's lie to keep her friends from asking

why she was leaving work so often. Even just hearing her lie spoken by someone she loved made Hazel's stomach clench, but it couldn't be helped. She kept telling herself it was for their own good.

"Fine. Wells is still being a jerk, but what's new," Hazel replied in her best casual voice, willing her hand not to shake as she reached for her coffee mug. She'd been so rattled, but it would be over in just a few more days. By the end of the week, she'd get the call from the doctor saying she was all clear and then life could get back to normal. No more lying and maybe she'd even be able to figure out what to do about Dylan, because what she was doing now wasn't working. She was miserable.

"He already has Chase living with him. Does he have to make it so permanent?" Callie said indignantly, for Hazel's sake. Hazel didn't deserve the defense, considering she was in the middle of a bald-faced lie. She'd have to apologize to Wells after all of this. She'd badmouthed him more in the past two weeks than during their entire divorce. But the only reason Hazel had thought up that would take so much time was if Wells tried to take legal custody of Chase. Well, besides the truth.

Beeping sounded, the same sound Hazel's alarm made every morning, causing her to jump and nearly spill her mug of coffee. Chills ran up her arms as she nervously pulled her phone out and stared at the screen. It was the ringtone she'd assigned to her doctor to make sure she didn't miss the call when it came. But now that it was here, she considered letting it go to voicemail. The call was early. She wasn't ready. Suddenly she wasn't so sure she was going to be getting good news. Why wasn't she sure? Was she getting some kind of premonition?

"Are you going to answer that?" Callie asked, causing Hazel to jump yet again.

She'd completely forgotten that Callie was in the room with

her. Hazel had never been so laser focused like she was on her phone now. Her phone that was still beeping.

"It could be the lawyer, right?" Callie asked.

No, it couldn't be. Because Hazel had lied, and after this call . . . she answered before the call could go to voicemail.

"Dr. Maddox?" Hazel no longer cared about her secret. She'd be telling her friends the truth after this call, one way or the other. Better for Callie to have some clues and start piecing together what Hazel had done.

Dr. Maddox? She saw Callie mouth the name and watched as her wheels began turning. Considering Dr. Maddox was the best OBGYN in town, Callie would have this all figured out in no time. Maybe she could tell the others the truth for Hazel.

"Hey, Hazel," Dr. Maddox said.

Hazel tried to read his tone. Did he sound sympathetic or relieved? Was he trying to soften the blow or was he ready to congratulate her?

"We've got your results," he continued.

Hazel held her breath.

Callie had moved close enough that she could hear everything the doctor was saying. There was no accusation in her face, just a look of concern as she met Hazel's gaze.

"I'm so sorry. It's cancer."

Cancer.

Cancer. The word continued on replay, causing Hazel's heart to clench and her hands to shake so much that she dropped the phone.

No, it couldn't be. This was just routine. She was supposed to be told it was a benign tumor, like Betty's. It wasn't supposed to be like this.

Callie gathered Hazel into her arms as she scooped up the phone and put it to her ear.

"Sorry, Dr. Maddox. This is Callie, Hazel's best friend." She held Hazel close with one arm and propped the phone against her ear with the other.

It wasn't until she was pressed against Callie's shirt and felt it become wet that Hazel realized she was crying. She felt devastated and yet numb at the same time.

"I understand," Callie said into the phone and then pulled it away from her ear.

"He has a few oncologist recommendations," Callie said softly. "Should I have him text them to you?"

Hazel nodded, or maybe she didn't. She didn't know. Her body felt out of her control.

"Do you mind texting those, Dr. Maddox?" Callie asked. After a pause she said, "Yes, I'll make sure she sets up an appointment immediately."

Callie was quiet for a few moments, the silence making all the more space for Hazel's tears. They'd come softly at first, but as more time passed, her cries became sobs that shook her to her core.

Hazel wasn't sure how long she cried in Callie's arms. She felt wrung out, as if there wasn't another drop of water in her, but every time she'd think the word *cancer* the tears would somehow be renewed.

"I'm so sorry, Hazel," Callie whispered, never letting her grip waver.

"Hazel, have you seen . . . ?" Kenzie opened Hazel's office door and poked her head in. She froze and muttered "What the hell?" as she took in the scene.

Hazel wasn't sure what or how Callie had communicated, but in another minute, Kenzie had joined Callie, wrapping her arms tightly around Hazel.

What could have been minutes or maybe hours later, Hazel's weeping began to quiet, and she realized she hadn't been alone in her tears. Pulling away from the hug, she saw that both of her friends' faces were damp and streaked with red tear tracks.

"I can't do this," Hazel said, her voice breaking at every word. Every part of her rebelled against that call, the diagnosis. But what was she to do now? The future had never felt so bleak and terrifying. She swallowed back yet another wave of fear. How long could she do this? How long would she survive? How much time did she have?

"You can and you will," Callie said, pulling Hazel back into the hug.

"And you won't be alone," Kenzie assured.

"Not for a single step," Callie agreed.

With those words, Hazel had the strength to swallow back yet another wave of paralyzing fear. She wasn't sure how she was going to do this. But she wasn't alone. For now, that had to be enough.

CHAPTER SIX

AT THE SOUND OF MOVEMENT, Laurel looked up from the computer behind the check-in desk. Kenzie and Callie wound their way through the lobby. Red eyes and barely-there smiles greeted her, all of them trying to remember their pact. They would not cry at work.

As hard as that pact had sounded when their best friend had just been diagnosed with cancer, living it was even harder.

Laurel knew Callie had her hands full with not only keeping up with her own work, but taking over all of Hazel's as well. On top of that, she'd hired an assistant to manage Hazel's social media accounts, and she had even started scheduling Hazel's doctor's appointments since she knew the doctor personally.

Callie had once sold a house to one of the best oncologists in northern California, and she'd cashed in on that personal relationship to land an appointment for Hazel the day after her diagnosis. Kenzie had been the one to go to the appointment with Hazel, and she'd relayed the news to the rest. Stage three. The cancer had not only spread to her lymph nodes under her right arm but it was also in the tissue. The good news was that the tumors were small, so it seemed that the cancer wasn't growing too quickly, although it was spreading. They'd all been hoping for a better prognosis but told themselves at least it wasn't stage four. Chemotherapy had been scheduled; the doctors hoped to shrink the cancer as much as possible before surgery and then radiation. It was a long road ahead.

But they weren't going to cry. At least at work. And when they were with Hazel. Ever since the phone call, they'd taken turns spending the evening with her, and it was Laurel's turn tonight. She planned on buying ingredients for Sterling's favorite meal before heading over. From her last visit, Laurel knew that Hazel didn't have much of an appetite but Sterling's was thriving.

"I have some news," Laurel said as her friends joined her at the check-in counter. Laurel and Kenzie had taken all of the shifts that their couple of part-time employees couldn't cover. Hopefully one day soon they'd be able to hire someone to work the desk full time, but right now that was an unneeded expense.

"Good news?" Kenzie asked hopefully.

Callie gripped the desk as if she already knew no news was good news these days. It felt like they'd been pummeled with a battering ram, and as they were trying to get up, they had been hit by a semi truck.

"I'll let you decide," Laurel said, rotating the computer screen so the others could see it.

There was a large photo of their Lodge on a social media page. It wasn't a page Hazel had set up.

"What's this?" Callie asked as she began to read.

Laurel watched as Callie's mouth dropped open and Kenzie's eyes narrowed in frustration.

"*This* is why we've been getting so many cancellations?" Kenzie asked, slamming a hand on the desk.

Laurel nodded. She'd found this page a few days before but

hadn't been able to figure out how they were spreading their misinformation. The person running the page had been brilliant, never using the words *Rosebud* and *Lodge* near one another. So on a normal Internet search, the page showed up so far down the list of websites that even Laurel hadn't gotten there in her searching. Not without the reverse image search she'd finally performed. Putting in a picture of the Lodge had been the only way for Laurel to find this page of lies. So how did customers who wouldn't even try to find this page come across it and the lies it was spreading?

As soon as she'd found the page, Laurel had done a search for *Rosebud Lodge* on the social media platform instead of in a search engine. Later that day, an ad had popped up. The headline claimed that the Rosebud girls had manipulated and stolen to get the land the Lodge sat on, appropriating it from a Native American tribe who insisted the ground was sacred to them. Basically, the ad stated that the girls had desecrated ancient burial grounds by building their Lodge.

It was ridiculous, considering that the land had belonged to a local family for generations and there was no record or even rumor that it had ever been used as a cemetery of any sort. No one other than greedy city council members had ever opposed the sale of the Lodge. Besides, the girls hadn't even built the Lodge or any of its outbuildings. But most prospective patrons wouldn't know that. And Laurel could imagine that as soon as they saw this vile accusation, they went right to Rosebud Lodge's website and canceled their reservations.

So Laurel had gone back to that first page and done some digging until she found all the ads. She thought she understood now what the person or people behind the smear campaign were doing. They catered the ads to people searching Rosebud Lodge on the social media platform along with another previously searched interest. One ad stated that one of the Lodge owners had previously run a puppy mill. Lies. Laurel guessed that ad went to people who loved animals and had searched the Lodge. Another was the burial ground one that Laurel had gotten. Laurel often searched groups that promoted human rights, so it made sense that she would have gotten that one. The last one seemed the vilest, and Laurel could hardly bring herself to read the whole thing. It claimed that the Lodge allowed members of a local human trafficking ring to use their rooms in their crimes. Just the thought of that made Laurel feel sick. She would have canceled her reservation as well, and maybe even called the cops.

Actually, Laurel was kind of surprised that hadn't happened yet. But then she looked at the date of that ad and saw it had only been running for two days. They might be hearing from local law enforcement soon.

"Crazy, right?" Laurel asked as her friends read. It was a lot to take in.

Kenzie just shook her head.

"I'm surprised the cops haven't been called on us," Laurel voiced her earlier thought.

"According to this ad, we're in the middle of an ongoing investigation, so they ask that no one disturb local law enforcement who are working so hard to put us criminals behind bars," Callie said, pointing to one of the posts. "This person is brilliant. An evil genius, but a genius nonetheless. All three of these things seem like a bit much, but they somehow wove a scenario where they all worked together and didn't seem completely fantastical. They've made it so people don't want to get involved but also don't feel threatened. If I didn't hate whoever this was or if they didn't hate me, I'd offer them a job."

"And they never put *Rosebud* and *Lodge* together," Laurel pointed out.

"Making it nearly impossible to find in an Internet search,

especially when we have so many other sites and links that would come up first and bury this one. They used our marketing and campaigning against us," Callie said.

"And look at this. I can't post. That's how they keep all of the information so streamlined," Kenzie said as she moved the mouse around the page.

"So now we know the why, but what do we do about it?" Callie asked.

Laurel had been proud that her work had finally produced something but was starting to feel that her find was just more bad news. If this information had led them somewhere, it would have been helpful. But just finding this page, and knowing someone was out there slandering them, did nothing.

"We could go to the cops?" She offered her one idea.

"Or to a lawyer?" Kenzie added.

"Riley Matthews killed it for Saff," Callie said thoughtfully.

The women sat silently thinking for a few moments.

"I have a few friends on the force, but I think I'd like to try Riley first," Callie added.

The other two nodded. It did seem like a safer bet.

"THIS IS . . . A LOT," Riley said as he looked over the page. Callie, Laurel, and Kenzie had gone to see him during his lunch break. When they'd called to schedule his next open appointment, they'd found he was booked for the next couple of weeks. But his secretary had talked to Riley personally, since she knew the women were his friends, and he'd offered to work through lunch to meet with them.

"And you have no idea who's behind it?" Riley asked.

Kenzie and Callie shook their heads in unison. Laurel sat motionless.

"Looks like you might have an inkling," Riley said, directing his question to Laurel.

"You saw how mad this town has been at my ex. Some of them think I'm guilty as well."

"Which she's not," Callie defended immediately.

Riley nodded. "I know. But I've also seen what Laurel is talking about. I could see someone being mad enough to do this. Especially since there's no way for anyone to take their anger out on Bennie right now."

Laurel hadn't even thought of that. With Bennie in jail and practically penniless, what more could be done to him? But if someone wanted to hurt him and saw Laurel starting to thrive, she could see why they'd want to sabotage her. Bennie had hurt a lot of people. Deeply.

"So what can we do?" Kenzie asked.

"File a police report. I doubt they'll do much with it, though. These kinds of cases are rough. Libel, which is what this is, is most likely to be tried in civil court. This is something you can sue for, not really a criminal act."

"It should be. It's practically stealing. These lies are ruining our business," Callie said.

Riley nodded. "The law isn't perfect. I, of all people, know that. But that's the way things work, at least for the time being, and I just do my best to make sure my clients get the best end of the deal. Even a crappy one."

Kenzie bit her lip, clearly deep in thought. Callie frowned. Laurel hated that she was the one who had basically put them all in this position.

"So we file a police report," Laurel said.

Riley nodded again. "It will help when we take this to court. Because we can, as soon as we find who's behind this. And oftentimes, hitting a person in civil court is just as hard of a hit as criminal court. Money talks."

Laurel knew Riley was attempting to make them feel better, and she had to admit it was kind of working.

"But the cops won't investigate?" Callie asked.

"Maybe a bit, but probably not much," Riley admitted. "They're typically overwhelmed, and if the prosecutor's office says they aren't likely to find enough evidence to take a solid case to court, which is almost certain for this situation, the police will often back off."

"That's messed up," Kenzie muttered.

"We've got an overworked system with too many loopholes," Riley agreed.

"So we hire someone?" Callie asked.

"That's one way. The other is for you to investigate on your own," Riley said.

"Yeah, we tried that. It got us here. And it now feels like a dead end." Laurel waved her hands in frustration.

"Do you have a suggestion for where we should go? Do we hire a computer guy?" Callie asked, leaning forward in her seat.

Kenzie chuckled.

"What? Do you know who we should hire?" Callie turned toward her hopefully, too anxious for action to be offended.

"No, you're right. A 'computer guy' sounds just right," Kenzie teased through her laughter.

Callie shook her head, refusing to laugh.

Riley looked from woman to woman, waiting for Kenzie's laughter to abate before speaking to Callie. "Probably not your neighborhood Geek Squad member, but yeah, a type of computer specialist could help you. Here's the contact info of someone I've worked with before. He's a bit strange, but he got the job done." Riley slid a business card across his desk to Laurel. "Once he figures out the identity of the person behind this page, you can bring it to me and I can take action. But until we have a perp, we're stuck."

The women nodded.

"Thank you, Riley," Callie said as she stood.

"Yeah, especially for taking your lunch break to do this," Kenzie added.

"This made the whole thing totally worth it," Riley said, pointing to the to-go container full of food Saffron had prepared for him.

"Not near what we owe you, but I guess it's a start?" Laurel said with a smile, the weight beginning to lift now that they had a direction to move. She felt one step closer to getting whoever was behind this and protecting her friends.

Callie and Kenzie walked out of the office, and Laurel was about to follow when Riley called after her, "Hey, Laurel. Do you have a second?"

She turned back to look at him. "Sure."

"Are you really doing okay?" He sounded genuinely concerned.

There were two types of people in town. At least that's what Laurel had learned since this mess with Bennie had started. The first hoped to pry gossip out of Laurel; the second truly cared and wanted to know how they could help. That second group was miniscule, but it seemed like Riley wanted to join. Laurel was always glad for another friend.

She nodded, reflecting. She still lived with Callie, but she had a job. She was doing something with her life after being a pampered housewife for years, so that felt good. Some may have thrived in the lavish lifestyle Laurel had previously led, but she found herself so much happier now, even without a husband and with the constant worry about money.

"I followed Bennie's trial, and I picked up that you feel some guilt for your part in what happened," Riley said. He stood, walking around his desk so that he was just a step or two away from Laurel.

Laurel's cheeks heated because Riley was right. And she wasn't sure she was ready for someone other than the girls to be able to read her so easily, especially someone she wasn't particularly close to. She and Riley had gone to high school together, but they hadn't really run in the same crowds. Riley had been smart, too smart to hang out with Laurel, and he'd also been well liked. He'd been friendly with nearly everyone—which was why each of the girls considered him a friend—but he hadn't been close to any of them.

"Don't," Riley said as he gently put a hand on Laurel's arm.

Laurel met his eyes, which were full of concern. Maybe not getting to know Riley better had been a mistake. He seemed like the kind of person anyone would be lucky to have in their corner.

"I work with men like Bennie daily, and they use whatever or whomever they can. Including their unsuspecting, beautiful wives," Riley said. He let go of her arm but stayed close, looking at her intently. "Bennie used you badly. He made the mistakes, not you."

"Then why does it feel like I did?" Laurel asked honestly. Maybe a little too honestly.

"Because you're kind and good and hate seeing people in this town hurt. Even if they don't deserve your compassion," Riley replied immediately, as if the answer were obvious. He hesitated and then continued, "I lost money I'd invested with Bennie."

Laurel's eyes went wide. She had no idea.

"I'm sorry," she whispered when she recovered from some of her shock.

Riley shook his head. "I'm not saying that for you to feel sorry for me. I'm saying that because a good number of Bennie's victims, me at the forefront, place none of the blame on you. You did nothing wrong," Riley stated firmly.

Laurel wanted to believe him.

"You're a good person, Laurel. Don't let Bennie's errors cloud that for you," Riley said softly.

Laurel stood frozen. Thoughts of all her mistakes flitted through her mind. But in the end, Riley was right. The choice had been Bennie's. She could have made completely different choices and the outcome would have been exactly the same.

"Thank you," Laurel whispered, clearing her throat and glancing around the room, embarrassed to meet his gaze.

Poor Riley. She'd become *that woman* that even her acquaintances felt they had to take care of.

"And thanks again for taking your lunch break . . . " Laurel's voice trailed off when she realized she was just repeating herself. But her heart was racing, and she was feeling things she shouldn't. At least not yet. She was still such a mess from her marriage. But feelings were happening, whether she wanted them to or not. She needed to get out of there before she lost control of her emotions.

"It's important to me that you know you have people on your side. I'm on your side," Riley said.

Laurel felt like she couldn't breathe.

What was she supposed to say? She took a step back and bumped against the still open door. But she couldn't just leave without responding, even if this conversation scared her. Even if what she was feeling terrified her. She couldn't have feelings for Riley. It made no sense. Granted, Laurel knew plenty of women who'd had these exact same flutterings for Riley. Now she'd joined them when she had no business doing so.

"Thank you," she said once again. The words felt inadequate, considering all Riley had done for her—the unnecessary kindness he had shown—but what more could she do? Maybe nothing at the moment. But she vowed then and there to figure out a way to right what Bennie had done to Riley and the others.

"You're welcome," Riley said genuinely before returning to his chair behind his desk.

That was Laurel's cue to get the heck out of there. She'd taken up way too much of his time. He was here being a good friend, and she was developing a crush like a teenager. Her cheeks warmed.

"And please keep me updated. If this guy finds anything, I'd love to represent you all," Riley said.

She nodded. "We'd appreciate that." Laurel made sure to say *we*. This wasn't something Riley was offering *her*; he was offering his aid to all of them. Her friends. People he'd been friendly with for years.

"And if you need anything, I'm here," Riley added.

What did that mean? Laurel was in no kind of headspace to investigate that offer, so she didn't. She just nodded, probably looking even sillier than she felt, before turning and leaving the office.

Just outside the open door stood Callie, with a huge grin on her face, and Kenzie, who pumped her eyebrows.

Laurel shook her head once, hoping her friends would keep quiet. For once.

They walked out of the office in silence, but as soon as they closed the lobby door and stood on the sidewalk, her friends rounded on her and both spoke at once.

"That was hot," Kenzie said.

Callie exuberantly added, "The town has speculated for ages why Riley has stayed single. Many say he's been in love with someone unavailable. It was you!"

Laurel shook her head. They were wrong. She had been ridiculous, and the interaction had been embarrassing. There was no hotness. And yeah, it was weird that a guy like Riley had never married, but he'd had plenty of girlfriends. The town was wrong—no way was he pining for someone. And Callie was doubly wrong—absolutely no way was Riley pining for Laurel.

"You just shake that lovely head and keep denying it, but you'll see the truth soon," Callie promised smugly.

Laurel held up the business card Riley had given her. "The only truth we'll be uncovering is who is behind our smear campaign. I'll call this guy as soon as we get back to the Lodge and hopefully we'll get things back to normal soon."

But even as she said the words, she knew that wouldn't truly be the case. With all that was going on with Hazel, she wondered if things would ever get back to normal.

"She'll be okay, right?" Laurel asked, and no one had to ask who she was talking about. Her friends' thoughts probably strayed to Hazel a dozen times a day, just as Laurel's did.

Callie nodded, jaw clenched. Kenzie said, "She has to be. She's too stubborn not to be."

The girls chuckled without much humor, but they were trying. Hazel wouldn't want them to be miserable.

"Mind if I join you guys tonight?" Callie asked Laurel, knowing it was Laurel's turn to check on Hazel.

"Me too?" Kenzie added before Laurel could respond.

"Of course not," Laurel said because she understood. Right now all she wanted was to be near Hazel, to see with her own eyes that her friend was okay, at least for the time being.

Callie and Kenzie sent her smiles of relief, and Hazel had a feeling Saffron would be joining them as well.

Everything seemed more manageable when they were together.

CHAPTER SEVEN

"I CAN'T," Alex said as he strode into the kitchen.

Saffron looked at him over her shoulder to respond with *what the heck are you talking about* but realized he was on the phone.

"New boss, my mom, the excuses are endless," Alex said with a laugh. "Besides, I've already been your best man three times."

Three times? Who was Alex speaking to, and why had this man gotten married so many times?

"Maybe I'm a bad-luck charm. Try a new best man this time. Or here's a novel idea. Be like every other woman and have a maid of honor," Alex teased.

It was easy to see he had a good relationship with whomever was on the other end of the call, and Saffron found herself caring way too much about who it was.

Especially now that she knew it was a woman.

She and Alex had been friendly since they'd had lunch together and buried their weapons of war, but that's all they were. Kitchen friends. Work buddies. They shared their days from nine to five, and after that they went their separate directions. Which was a good thing.

Or so Saffron kept telling herself. Especially when she found herself wanting to ask what Alex was doing after work. Did he want to grab dinner? A drink? A movie?

She focused on the pasta salad she was preparing for the day's special. That was where her attention needed to be. Not on why her relationship with Alex wasn't progressing and definitely not on the woman on the other side of the call.

"I really am sorry I can't be there, Kels. I'll try harder next time," Alex promised jokingly. The laughter on the other end of the call was so loud Saffron could hear it from where she stood.

She heard a rustling sound and guessed Alex was putting his phone away before washing his hands. A minute later, he joined her at the counter with an easygoing smile.

It was still early; she and Alex were the only ones who came in at this time. While the Lodge was still dealing with cancellations, Saffron had decided to only serve lunch. So far it had been working well for them, but she'd had to let a few of her cooks go. It hurt, but it was better for the restaurant's bottom line. She had to look out for the investment she and her friends had made. She'd assured the cooks that as soon as she was able to rehire, they'd be the first people she called. Hopefully, she'd be able to do so soon.

"What do you need me to do, Boss?" Alex sounded pretty upbeat, considering he'd just let down a friend. But that was Alex. He wasn't just happy when he dodged the punches—even when he got hit he kept going, cheerful as ever.

"Do you want to start grinding the meat for the burger patties?" Saffron asked sweetly.

It was probably the job she should have started with, but she hated grinding meat and Alex didn't mind it, so she often left the task to him.

Alex chuckled. "Sure."

He left the room, heading toward the fridge where the meat was stored, and then set up on the station just across from Saffron.

Saffron fixed her attention on adding the ingredients to her dish, and the two worked in comfortable silence.

See, they were friends. Saffron could totally ask him who he'd been speaking to. A friend being married four times was the kind of story work buddies shared, right? Right.

"So, your side of that call sounded interesting," she said before she could lose her nerve.

"That's life with Kels. Things are definitely interesting," Alex said, piling chunks of steak and pork into the grinder. It was Saffron's proprietary blend and made the best burgers ever, if she did say so herself. She had the awards to prove it.

"Kels. Is that someone from high school?" Saffron knew she was prying but couldn't help it. She was dying to know who this woman was.

Alex shook his head. "I met her in culinary school in LA. Cooking was her passion . . . at the time. Her passions change nearly as often as her husbands."

Saffron giggled because she knew it was the right response to make, but hoped it wouldn't keep Alex from continuing. She had a feeling the story was just getting good.

"We got married two months after we met," Alex continued calmly.

Saffron dropped her spoon. Thankfully it hadn't been a knife.

"Married?" Saffron stuttered, her eyes wide.

"Yeah, Kels was my first wife," Alex replied, as if he were telling her old news.

He wasn't.

And *first* wife? That meant there had to at least be a second, didn't it?

"The marriage only lasted a couple of months, and we divorced before we even finished school," Alex added as Saffron struggled not to choke on the spit she'd sucked in when she'd gasped.

"And she's asking you to be her best man?" Saffron had so many questions.

Alex chuckled. "Yeah, that's Kels for you. She liked to tell people at each of her subsequent weddings that I was her some-thing old."

It was kind of funny. If this woman wasn't Alex's ex-wife, she and Saffron would probably be friends. Wait, what did her being Alex's ex have to do with anything? Of course she and Saffron would be friends. If Kels lived in Rosebud. Yeah, that was the problem.

"And you were married again after that?" Saffron prodded.

"Yup. My second and final marriage," Alex said.

Saffron wasn't sure why her heart dropped at the word *final*. The last thing she'd dreamed of was marrying Alex. Okay, maybe not the last thing, but the thought hadn't even crossed her mind.

Oh man, she was sick of lying to herself.

Fine, the thought had crossed her mind. But it hadn't been a serious thought. She'd just wondered *what if*. And now she knew it would never happen. She should be thankful for Alex's admission. No point pining for a man who would never marry again.

"Who was your second wife?" Saffron asked, hoping it wouldn't sound awkward to go back to the conversation after the silence.

"Olive."

What kind of name was Olive? Were her parents obsessed with pizza? Popeye?

"I met her during my first job, right out of school. I was working at this crazy kitchen in Laguna. She walked in, and I was a goner. We got married a few weeks later, and I was a terrible husband. She left me, and I couldn't even blame her. I decided then and there I wasn't husband material."

"Wasn't that, like, twenty years ago?" Saffron asked.

Alex nodded.

"So couldn't you have changed?"

"If anything, I've become worse. More set in my ways, more addicted to my job. Nope. I won't do that to a woman again. Especially a woman I claim to love," Alex said. He peeled off his gloves and began to clean up his station. "You know what it's like."

Saffron nodded absently and went into the fridge to get the ingredients for the two pasta sauces she was preparing.

Was that why she had never settled down? Sure, she'd dated. A lot. But things had never progressed into long relationships. She'd either gotten bored or—Alex was right—the men in Saffron's life complained that they came second to her job. She'd assumed it was a male ego thing, but maybe she'd been too quick to judge. Maybe she and her job were at fault.

But things were different now. She could feel it. This job was slower paced and she had time to open up her life. She spent every Sunday with her family and sometimes went to her mom's midweek too. Although she'd seen her mom less in the past few weeks because she'd spent as many evenings as she could at Hazel's.

Thinking about Hazel made Saffron sick to her stomach. She couldn't imagine what her friend was going through. With an effort she pushed the thoughts away. Hazel had told her to focus on work at work and quit worrying so much. Saffron often wondered who was comforting whom when she went to Hazel's. She tried to be strong and lighthearted, but Hazel often ended up talking Saffron out of her melancholy. The woman couldn't help but be the rock for the rest of them, even when she was the one in trouble. The definition of strong.

So she was going to take Hazel's advice and concentrate on work. And maybe just a little on Alex. She had a feeling Hazel would approve of that.

"So why can't you be Kels's best man this time?" Saffron asked, lugging a huge tub of ingredients out of the fridge.

She was done discussing their ability to be good spouses. She had a feeling she wouldn't like the result of that conversation, since she still desired to get married, and a tiny, silly part of her continued to hold onto hope that the man she ended up with could be Alex. Absurd. Ridiculous. And yet it wouldn't leave.

"You mean, besides the fact that my boss is a tyrant?" Alex asked as he disassembled the grinder to clean all of its nooks and crannies. The worst part of the job, by far.

"Yeah," Saffron said, dumping ingredients onto the counter with more force than necessary. She had to admit that Alex was right. Saffron probably wasn't the best of bosses, and she did work them both too hard. Besides, didn't the greatest bosses take the worst tasks? She winced as she watched Alex cleaning the grinder.

"You know I'm joking, right? I really like working for you," Alex said. He paused, waiting until she met his eyes.

"I'm making you clean the grinder alone. Pretty sure that makes me kind of a tyrant," Saffron said, shrugging uncomfortably.

Alex returned to his work. "Well, then, I guess I like working for a tyrant."

Saffron felt her heart warm and chided it immediately. That

was barely a compliment. She couldn't let her heart flutter over something so ridiculous. Stubbornly, it kept right on fluttering, ignoring her sensible demands.

"The wedding is in LA," Alex continued, completely oblivious to Saffron's silly heart. Thankfully. "It's a whole thing: rehearsal dinner the night before, huge ceremony, and then reception. I'd have to be down there for three days, and I can't leave my mom that long." Alex moved the pieces of the grinder to the nearest sink.

"Doesn't she have a caretaker?" Saffron asked. She could've sworn Alex had said something along those lines.

Alex nodded. "But I try to give the caretaker at least every other evening off. It's a lot for one person to take on."

She had to imagine it was a lot for Alex as well, but he'd never complained about needing to be there for his mom. She was the only family he had, thanks to a car accident that had claimed the lives of his dad, sister, and nephew. It had been one of the greatest tragedies in Rosebud history.

Saffron was also willing to bet that because Alex's family had become so small, his ex who insisted on inviting him to her weddings was probably still part of that group. Or at least a really close friend. It would be a shame for Alex to miss a semi-important event in her life. Saffron would have called any other person's wedding a huge event, but it seemed like Kels didn't take them very seriously, if this was her fourth. Or was it fifth? Saffron had already lost track.

"She's marrying some movie producer, and they're inviting half the city. Basically, she'll be fine on the best man front. She'll have plenty of friends clamoring for the position. Asking me was just kind of tradition."

"A tradition you like?" Saffron asked.

Alex shrugged as he disinfected the counter and started forming the burger patties. "I guess? It's weird that she's gotten married so many times, but I guess I do like that we've stayed close enough that she asks me to be in her wedding party. It makes me feel less like a failure at the whole relationship thing."

Saffron nodded in understanding. She didn't have that kind of a relationship with any of her exes, but if she did she'd be proud of it.

"Then you should go," she said.

Alex shook his head. "Thanks, but I know you need me here."

"I can handle one weekend without you. We can ask Paul to take the extra shifts. He'd love it."

Alex pursed his lips. He knew it was the truth.

"And I can stay with your mom for a couple of nights," Saffron added quickly, speaking before Alex could refuse her offer, but also before she really thought through what she was doing. Could Saffron spend that much time with Alex's mom? Was it smart for her to get more involved in the life of this man who was so off limits?

"I don't know . . . " Alex hesitated.

Saffron knew she should be grateful he was letting her off the hook. This was a terrible idea. But she felt slightly offended at the same time. Did he not think she was capable of taking care of his mom?

"I can hang out with her," Saffron reiterated. It was a small task, something she could do after work. Not a big deal. Other than the whole becoming part of Alex's personal life thing. Something she'd just told herself wasn't a good idea.

"It's not that. I think you'd be great with my mom. Basically, all she needs is someone to talk to so she doesn't get lonely. She's still doing pretty well, considering. Her memory isn't always the greatest, but she can still mostly take care of herself. I usually make her dinner and make sure she doesn't fall and stuff," Alex said. Saffron was pretty sure she could handle that.

"But you have so much going on with Hazel and your friends," he added.

So that was why he was concerned. That was sweet. And even though Saffron probably should take the out Alex offered, she wouldn't. In the end, no matter what could or couldn't be between them, she wanted him to be happy. And she thought going to this wedding would make him happy.

"They'll be fine without me for a couple of nights. If anything, I think Hazel is sick of hearing me complain about my trial of my best friend having cancer," Saffron said, pleased that she was able to joke about the situation. This was a big moment for her. Hazel would have been so proud.

Alex laughed, thrilling Saffron to her core. She loved that sound.

She shook her head to clear that thought, which was much more than friendly, and focused on the task at hand.

"When is the wedding?"

"Next weekend," Alex replied.

Saffron's eyes widened. It was a little late to be finding a best man.

"Are you sure you weren't a last-minute replacement?" she asked, skeptical that a wedding of the magnitude Alex had described could leave such a big detail unaccounted for until so close to the big day.

"She just got engaged last month but decided she wanted to get married ASAP. Not sure why, but when Kels gets an idea she runs with it, and everyone just has to go along with it. This one has been practically a hurricane, or at least that's what she said her mom calls it. With so little time, she focused on everything else because she knew one of the last things she needed to do was ask me to be her best man since I already had a tux, thanks to her other three weddings. Well, four, if you count my own. So yeah, it was a fast turnaround. But it's amazing what money can do. Especially the kind of money Kels's new fiancé has."

"That's insane." Saffron shook her head, feeling exhausted just listening.

"That's Kels," Alex replied with a shrug.

"So, next weekend," Saffron muttered as she pulled out her phone, checking her calendar to make sure she wasn't making a commitment she couldn't keep. But sure enough, her phone showed she was free next Friday through Sunday. Tuesday was the date of Hazel's first chemo treatment, but until then, Saffron was completely free. In fact, having something to keep her busy while she waited for Tuesday would be helpful.

"I'm in," Saffron said, slipping her phone into the back pocket of her black jeans.

"Are you sure?" Alex asked in the way people do when they feel the need to protest but also really hope you'll say yes.

"I'm sure," Saffron said, and the words were barely out before Alex ran around their stations and pulled her into his arms.

"You are the best. I knew you'd be the greatest friend if you could just stop hating me," he said, laughing and trying to keep his messy hands off her clothes.

Saffron tried to laugh along. Right, *friend*. Because that's what they were, and Alex's friend zone was where she'd always be.

———

"HELLO? MRS. GRANGER?" Saffron called out as she knocked and then opened the door to the home Alex shared with his mom.

Alex had given her a key when he'd stopped by that morning. He was planning to catch a flight out of San Francisco down to LA instead of driving the seven hours so that he could be away from his mom for as short a time as possible.

"Hey, you must be Saffron." A cute woman in tie-dyed scrubs entered the foyer and led Saffron into the kitchen.

"And you're Aja?" Saffron asked the nurse, who nodded in response.

"I thought I should bring you in here before introducing you to Mrs. Granger. She's had several really great days in a row, but our luck stopped today. I decided against calling Alex because this lapse in memory isn't anything I can't handle. But I thought I should let you know what's going on before leaving you two alone. If it seems like more than you can handle, I'll stay here tonight and have Alex home by morning," Aja said.

Alex would be on the next flight back if he knew his mother wasn't doing well. But Saffron didn't want that for him. Hadn't she done this so that he could enjoy freedom from his obligations for a couple of days? If Saffron could handle this, she would.

"I'd like to hear what being with Mrs. Granger would entail before we make that decision," Saffron said, trying to hide the wariness she felt.

"Oh, being with her wouldn't be difficult. She still has complete ability to care for herself. Alex told you that, right?"

He had, but the phrase *our luck stopped* had worried Saffron. She just nodded.

"What I meant by a bad day is that she's more forgetful than she's been in recent days. For example, she forgot to turn off the stove after cooking a pot of soup. She still remembered every ingredient in the soup, but the minor task of turning off the burner was neglected. It just means I have to keep a closer eye on her."

That Saffron could totally do. Honestly, it sounded a lot like spending time with one of her brothers. They were constantly forgetting important things that Saffron followed behind them to fix . . . even as grown men.

"And the other thing is that she's slipping back into the past. Not for long periods of time, but she'll have moments where she'll forget the year, forget who I am, think that she's back in Alex's childhood," Aja explained.

"Oh." Saffron hadn't realized that Mrs. Granger's disease had already progressed to that point. She didn't know much about Alzheimer's, but she did know that each case developed uniquely. She couldn't imagine how difficult this part of the illness had been for Alex. It had to feel like losing a part of his mom every time this happened. Saffron was even more thankful that she'd told Alex to leave. Hopefully, his mom would be back to better days by the time he got home.

"This lapse could last for the next ten minutes, the rest of the night, the week, or forever," Aja explained.

This was why Alzheimer's was so cruel. It stole indiscriminately and unpredictably.

"Do you think you'll be okay?" Aja asked.

Saffron nodded. At the moment she wasn't sure, but she was determined to grin and bear whatever these next two evenings brought. She wanted to do this for Alex.

"Then let me introduce you to Mrs. Granger. You may have to remind her of who you are from time to time, but it will be good to have an initial introduction anyway," Aja said with a smile that said she felt confident in Saffron's ability to do this.

Saffron wished she felt as confident.

She followed Aja from the kitchen into the living room. Mrs. Granger sat on the couch, her eyes fixed on a television. A TV tray was in front of her, and on it rested a bowl of the soup Saffron assumed she'd made earlier.

"What is the Louisiana Purchase," Mrs. Granger said in unison with the contestant on the TV.

"She's somehow retained most of the trivia knowledge she's been famous for knowing. The woman is a wonder," Aja whispered before saying in a louder voice, "Mrs. Granger, I want you to meet someone."

Alex had wanted to introduce Saffron to his mom the evening before, while he was still in town, but Saffron's nephew had a school event and she couldn't miss it. By the time that was over, Mrs. Granger had been asleep, so Saffron had assured him that she'd be fine coming over without an introduction from Alex as long as the nurse hadn't left before Saffron arrived. It had seemed like a great idea up until this point. Now that she was about to meet Alex's mom, she was second-guessing everything.

"Who is it?" Alex's mom asked, turning in her seat.

Saffron had not expected the strong alto that came out of Mrs. Granger's mouth. She didn't know why she'd assumed the woman's voice would be frail, but she'd been wrong. She made a mental note to stop assuming things about Mrs. Granger in the future.

"I'm Saffron, a friend of Alex's." She stepped out from behind Aja and held out her hand.

It was time for her to stop being timid. She was going to do this, and she was going to do it well. Mrs. Granger, Aja, and Alex deserved that from her.

"Nice to meet you, Saffron," Mrs. Granger said, grasping her hand firmly. The woman might look like she weighed a hundred pounds sopping wet, but she had more strength than her small frame indicated. "I love meeting Alex's friends. Where is Alex?"

Saffron looked to Aja for guidance. The sweet nurse smiled and nodded so Saffron decided to tell the truth.

"He went to a wedding," she explained.

Mrs. Granger chuckled. "My boy is definitely a romantic."

Alex a romantic? Really? But Mrs. Granger had already moved on.

"Saffron, hm. Are you the Saffron Alex goes to school with?" Mrs. Granger asked.

Apparently they were back in Alex's teenaged years. Coping with that should be a little less difficult, considering Saffron had known Alex during that time. Sure, they had hated one another all through high school, but that meant Saffron had known almost as much about him as she had her friends. She believed in keeping her enemies close.

Of course, Alex insisted he hadn't hated Saffron then, but she still wasn't convinced. No one spent so much time playing pranks on someone else unless they strongly disliked them.

"I am," Saffron answered honestly.

"I'm so glad the two of you could bury that silly hatchet. Poor Alex really is foolish when it comes to the girls he likes," Mrs. Granger said.

Saffron inhaled so quickly she choked on the air. She coughed, mentally replaying Mrs. Granger's words. That couldn't possibly be right. In recent years, Callie had teased Saffron that Alex had always liked her, and even Saffron's mother had implied it, but they didn't know Alex.

His mom did though. And she was saying the same thing. Saffron held onto the couch for support, struggling to take it in. To think that the boy who had teased her mercilessly had done it because he liked her? Impossible.

She had to admit, though, that he'd never been cruel or even mean. His teasing had always been good-natured, but Saffron hadn't been relaxed enough back in high school to take even the tamest of jokes. More and more, she was seeing the past in a different light, and honestly, she didn't like the way this new brightness showed just how immature she had been.

Saffron's favorite book back in the day had been *Anne of*

Green Gables but she'd never expected to live out the romantic plot of the story. Had Alex been her Gilbert Blythe? Her heart sputtered at the thought.

"Yeah, but we're just friends," Saffron insisted, unable to allow Mrs. Granger—or herself—to think anything but the truth. She and Alex had buried the hatchet, but even if he had felt that way about her once upon a time, they were friends now. Just friends. She reigned in her hopes sternly.

"Maybe for now, but if I know my Alex, he won't let a good girl like you go," Mrs. Granger said knowingly.

Saffron knew she couldn't set her heart on anything Mrs. Granger said. Her illness was playing tricks on her. But the compliments were nice, and Saffron had a feeling she was truly going to enjoy her time with this sweet woman.

CHAPTER EIGHT

HAZEL SWALLOWED as she took her first steps out of the car. Wells had dropped her at the front door of the hospital, where Callie had been waiting, immediately taking Hazel's arm and directing her to where she needed to be.

They said in times of crisis you could know who your people were, and boy, had Hazel's people showed up.

Wells had dropped everything, and had flown into San Francisco with Chase the very day Hazel had told him of her prognosis. She hadn't expected her ex to do so—she'd really expected very little from him—but he'd insisted. When they divorced he'd said he wanted to be there for their boys, and Hazel could believe that. But then he would do things like flying across the country to drive her to the hospital, and she'd wonder.

Granted, since Wells was staying in her home with their boys it made sense for him to drive. But Hazel was a bit confused, wondering about her relationship with her ex. Were they now . . . friends?

She had to admit that would be nice, being friends with her greatest foe. Especially now.

One of her first decisions after her diagnosis had been to get rid of negativity in her life. She didn't have the time, space, or emotional bandwidth for that. If she was going to fight and beat this cancer—which she would—she needed to go into battle with a bright outlook.

This new bright outlook didn't keep her from crying herself to sleep most nights. But no one, not even Hazel, was expecting perfection. She was doing her best, taking one step at a time and trying not to let fear, negativity, or defeat take over. She sometimes allowed them a brief, starring role in her emotions, but then she'd kick them back out.

She and Callie took slow steps toward the elevators, where they would go up three floors to the oncology ward. There she'd be checked in for her first chemotherapy treatment.

Chills swept over Hazel's body from head to toe. She'd never imagined being in a situation like this. But she appreciated that they had a plan in place. Her cancer was treatable; she could be saved. One day, she *would* be cancer-free, and Hazel was determined to make it to that day.

Callie opened her mouth as if she were going to say something, but then closed it. Hazel didn't blame her. What was there to say? They both knew Hazel had everything she needed and they both knew Hazel wasn't okay. What else could she ask?

As they rode the elevator in silence, Hazel thought about the road ahead of her. Chemo was just the start. After the tumor shrank she would have surgery, followed by radiation. Her body was about to start the struggle of a lifetime, but Hazel was doing her best to be prepared.

They stepped out of the elevator and as Hazel took in her surroundings, her feet refused to move. Despite all of her thoughts and words on positivity, this—standing and seeing the oncology department, the nurses waiting for her—was all too real.

"I can't," she whispered.

Callie held her arm a little tighter. "You can and you will," she assured her best friend.

Hazel nodded shakily as the ding of the elevator alerted her that someone else was getting off on this floor.

Voices she recognized came to her ears as the doors opened, and people spilled out.

Sterling and Chase were followed by Wells. Kenzie, Bryan, Saffron, and Laurel seemed to emerge all four at once, followed by Hazel's parents and her brother, Roger. Hazel's smile finally made a true appearance. She'd never felt more loved.

"We've got you," Callie reiterated.

Hazel knew they did.

"But what about the Lodge?" Hazel asked when she realized everyone was here with her.

"Alex," Saffron said.

"Our employees can handle a day alone," Kenzie added.

Hazel guessed they could.

As she smiled at her support network, she suddenly noticed a huge gap. Dylan's absence was hard to miss and her heart ached suddenly.

But she'd pushed him away. She'd told him not to come and had warned all of her friends and family not to give him any details. He needed to move on with his life, not be stuck on this ride with her when they weren't committed yet. He could get out and find a girlfriend who wasn't a mom of two, with an ex the world loved, and who now had cancer.

As much as she knew that, Hazel's heart called for the man she'd grown to adore. But it was too late. The time for her to step up was here, and she had plenty of people to help her through it without Dylan.

Her boys gathered her in a hug, and Hazel grinned. They were here for her; they believed in her. And she wasn't about to let any of these people down. Hazel had heard horror stories about chemo that had made her blood run cold, but now none of that mattered. Chemo was a tool to help her fight this ugly disease. She would use it, wield it, and come out the victor.

"Bring it on," Hazel said, and her friends and family cheered in approval.

———————

AND THEN THAT first shot of poison filled her body. Tears had fallen down Hazel's cheeks as Callie held her hand.

They'd left the rest of the group in the waiting room, and Hazel had been glad. With Callie, she didn't have to pretend.

Hazel had kept her positivity and resolution to get through this with a smile until just before that IV had begun to invade her body. But then the cold liquid had hit her. Putting something so toxic into her body just felt wrong. It was going to literally kill parts of her. Yet she was doing this willingly, because it was her best option for life.

She had to try to live for her boys, her friends, her parents. The list of people who mattered to her was long, and as much as Hazel wanted to be grateful for that long list, when she left the hospital six hours later, she felt she had nothing more to give the world. As the poison had filled her body, it felt like more than just hair follicles and cells had been obliterated. She felt so weak, like too much that was vital to her had been taken. And this was just session one.

She had to go through this seven more times. Fear clawed at her throat. It had been so much easier to be positive, to say she could kick cancer's butt, before she'd endured that first session. Before she'd known what sitting in that hospital room would feel like.

Now, she honestly didn't know if she would survive. But she had to.

She'd asked Wells to take the boys home after they'd come into the room to see her one hour into her treatment. She didn't want her boys to see her in that hospital bed again. Once had been one time too many, an IV filling her with a liquid that was her one salvation and yet would leave her to suffer terrible consequences.

Hazel's parents and brother had been the next to go. Hazel had insisted that she had her friends and there was no need for them to sit and worry over her. Her mother had wanted to stay, but she was nearing eighty and didn't need this kind of extra hardship. Still, only after Callie had insisted she would take care of Hazel would her family leave.

And then the girls had gone, except for Callie. Hazel had nothing left to give them. They tried to entertain her, but Hazel could barely find the strength to listen and watch. She just wanted it all to be over.

"You were amazing," Callie insisted as she drove Hazel home.

Darkness had descended while they were in the hospital. It seemed appropriate for how Hazel felt.

She'd had to be taken to the car in a wheelchair. She also had one waiting at home, even though she'd been sure she would never need it. But Wells had insisted they buy one so they could be prepared for any scenario. Thanks to him, it was waiting, and Hazel wouldn't have to walk at all. Wells and Callie had been miracle workers, getting everything Hazel could possibly need, and even helping to move her into the downstairs bedroom so she wouldn't have to navigate the stairs for the foreseeable future.

But right now, she didn't even have it in her to be grateful.

The vibration of the car was doing nothing to help the

nausea from the chemo, and her entire body felt betrayed by what she had just inflicted on it.

She held a bag to her chest just in case that nausea took over.

Thankfully, she lived close to Rosebud General, and it was only a few minutes before Callie was turning into the driveway. Hazel was finally home.

The light in the car came on as Hazel's door opened from the outside. She turned to see whether Wells, or maybe Sterling or Chase, was waiting for her.

But the forest-green eyes that greeted her didn't belong to any of them.

"Dylan?" Hazel asked, still too weak to do more than whisper.

What was he doing here? Why was he here? How did he know? But those words were too much, and she was too spent to utter them. She was just glad to see him.

She felt him unbuckle her seat belt and lift her into his arms, and was enveloped by a feeling of safety and security she hadn't even realized she'd been missing.

"Careful. I might puke on you," Hazel managed to say as she held onto her vomit bag.

"It's a risk I'm willing to take," Dylan whispered, softly pressing his lips to Hazel's forehead.

"Everything hurts," Hazel revealed without meaning to. But her blanket of safety made her speak things she'd promised to keep to herself.

"I know," Dylan said. In the moonlight she saw tears glittering in his eyes.

"We've got a wheelchair," Hazel heard Wells say.

"I've got her," Dylan responded, holding her just a little closer. The tone of his voice didn't allow for any argument.

"Is that what Hazel wants?" Callie said, not one bit intimidated by Dylan.

"Yes," Hazel said, surprising herself. She'd been so sure she was right to let Dylan go, but now all she wanted was to be wrapped in his arms. It was selfish, and she would evaluate things later. But right now, she would allow herself this moment.

"He's been waiting in his car for hours. I told him to head out, but he doesn't listen so well," Wells said. Hazel wasn't sure who he was talking to. Her head was against Dylan's chest, her eyes closed.

"How did you know it was today?" Callie asked the question Hazel had been wondering as well.

Hazel felt Dylan move. She was guessing he was shaking his head.

"If I reveal my secrets, you'll dam the information source," Dylan replied.

"Touché," Callie said, sounding impressed.

Hazel kind of was too.

"I didn't think you'd want the boys around, so I sent them to Sterling's friend's house for the night," Wells said, probably to Hazel.

"Thank you," Hazel said softly even though what she really wanted to ask was how Wells had managed to get Chase to go with Sterling. In the past, her older son had always acted as though he was too good for Sterling's friends. But however Wells had done it, Hazel was glad. She hadn't wanted her boys to see her so weak.

The lights of the house burned even behind Hazel's closed eyes, and she shifted, pressing her face against Dylan's hard chest.

"Do you want to turn some of those off?" Dylan asked.

Suddenly the light wasn't so glaring.

"I've just got the lamp on in here," Wells said. His voice was getting louder as Dylan walked, so Hazel knew they must be getting closer to her room.

Suddenly she was enveloped in her blankets, her soft mattress at her back. She was carefully tucked in, and she felt rather than saw the presence of Wells, Callie, and Dylan at her bedside.

"I'm leaving your phone by your bed, just in case you need anything. I can be here in minutes," Callie promised.

"Or you could always call me," Wells said. There was a hint of gruffness in the low voice he was famous for crooning with. "I'm only a minute away, being upstairs and all."

"None of that is necessary," Dylan concluded, "because I'm staying right here."

Hazel's eyes flew open.

"Didn't she break up with you, man? Just head home. We've got this." Wells pointed back and forth between Hazel and his chest.

Hazel's quick movement, however minor, had been a mistake. Her stomach heaved, and she pulled the bag she thankfully still held up to her mouth.

Several moments of retching later, the bag was removed and replaced with a bowl. She knew the hands caring for her better than she should, considering the short time they'd dated.

Only after the nausea had fully subsided did Hazel look up.

Callie stood waiting with a wet towel. She handed it to Hazel as Dylan took her bowl full of puke.

"I'm sorry," she began as she watched Dylan take it.

"Don't even start with that. I'm not sorry at all," he said as he turned and left the room.

Hazel realized only Callie was still with her. She felt slightly better after throwing up, but she had a feeling the relief would be short lived. Her head still ached, and her body was still cold.

"Wells?" she asked, her voice raspy.

"Left as soon as the puking started," Callie said.

Hazel wasn't surprised. Anytime the boys had caught a stomach bug, it had been her job to nurse them back to health. Wells had claimed to have a weak stomach. Hazel remembered thinking bitterly that almost everyone had weak stomachs when it came to cleaning up vomit, but most people pushed through it when someone was in need. Wells was weak in that area as well.

Although that really wasn't fair. He'd been so good to her lately, being the exact friend she'd needed. She was determined to let go of any negative feelings regarding Wells from their marriage and divorce and remember that he'd stepped up when she really needed him.

Hazel used the warm washcloth to clean herself as best she could and then handed it back to Callie.

"Before he gets back, I need to know. Do you want me to fight this Dylan thing?" Callie met Hazel's eyes searchingly.

Did she? She was pretty sure that if left with just Wells she wouldn't have managed these last few minutes well. But was it fair to use Dylan as a nurse?

"Even if she does, I'm not going anywhere," Dylan said, entering the room with the same bowl he'd taken out a few minutes ago, freshly washed.

Oh heavens, he'd cleaned her puke. If Hazel weren't feeling so terribly, that would have been a concern. But right now she just wanted to go to sleep. With Dylan nearby.

She was selfish. She was self-centered. She was a terrible person. But she'd have to deal with that later.

"Okay." Hazel knew she was giving in too fast. But she wouldn't risk saying anything that might make Dylan leave. She loved her tribe, but she needed Dylan.

"Okay," Callie agreed, and Hazel swore she was biting back a grin.

"I love you," Callie added. She kissed the top of Hazel's head and quietly left the room.

"We've got this." Wells was suddenly back.

"Felt it was safe since Callie left? Figured the puke must be done, right?" Dylan's voice had changed from tender to confrontational. His body shifted, subtly moving between Hazel and Wells.

"If no one else was here, I would have taken care of it," Wells countered.

"Bro, just let me take care of my girlfriend," Dylan said, shaking his head in disgust.

"Ex-girlfriend," Wells corrected, taking a step closer.

Hazel had had enough. She knew what she wanted.

"Thanks, Wells. You've done enough. Dylan can cover the rest." She tried to sound diplomatic, given that they were both her exes.

Hazel closed her eyes, her nausea returning. She needed sleep. Anything to escape how she felt.

Even with her eyes closed, she recognized Dylan's hands. Maybe it was his scent, or the careful way he pulled the blankets back over her and nestled her into her pillows.

Hazel finally fled into the bliss of unconsciousness.

CHAPTER NINE

"RAQUEL!" It took everything in Kenzie to refrain from screaming her sister's name.

But she'd promised.

Kenzie looked around her home, heartsick and angry. The typically pristine surroundings were a mess. And that was putting it nicely.

Clothes, hopefully clean, were strewn all over the living room floor, dishes were piled haphazardly in the sink, and a potted plant had been tipped over, spilling dirt onto the entryway tile. Not to mention the dog hair that covered every single surface. Three huge, hairy dogs equaled no end of shedding.

And Kenzie had put up with it all for days without a single complaint. She'd even grown to appreciate cuddles from Justin, Mark, and Nick. Leave it to Raquel to name her dogs after three of her favorite boy band members. But Bryan was coming over for dinner that evening. They were supposed to have a quiet night at home. Raquel had promised to put her dogs in the yard for the day and to clean up the hair so Bryan wouldn't have a major allergy attack just stepping foot into the home he should have still been sharing with Kenzie.

"Raquel!" This time Kenzie did shout, because her sister hadn't answered.

Instead of her sister's footsteps, the sound of twelve paws skittering against her hardwood floors hit Kenzie's ears.

She braced herself as Nick, followed by Mark and Justin, came barreling into her. Thankfully, the wall caught her fall.

So her sister had done absolutely nothing she'd promised.

But that wasn't the dogs' fault.

Kenzie knelt to give all three boys big hugs and scratches and let them lick her face. She did everything she could to keep her lips away from their tongues. She wasn't quite to the point of actually returning a dog's kisses yet.

After she'd sufficiently loved on the dogs—they really were adorable—she stood to find her sister. The dogs were growing on her, but her sister? Kenzie drew in a deep breath. She loved Raquel. But they were so different. Her parents and friends had tried to warn her, but Kenzie hadn't listened—partially because she'd hoped Raquel had grown up a bit from the last time she'd seen her, but mostly because Kenzie had been lonely. She hadn't even been willing to admit this to herself, but now she realized it.

Maybe she could blame all of this on Bryan?

She smiled at the thought but dismissed it. Kenzie had invited her sister to live with her, and these were the consequences.

Kenzie walked into the guest wing of her home, yelling Raquel's name all along the way. No answer.

But she'd seen Raquel's car in the driveway when she'd gotten home, so she had to be here.

Kenzie finally turned toward her own bedroom, and as she

entered, she heard her shower running. Seriously? She had one rule for her sister: leave her master bedroom alone.

Ugh. Kenzie fought to keep from shrieking, but her head was filled with a piercing pain that only occurred when she was this frustrated with Raquel.

The water stopped, and the shower door opened.

"Raquel," Kenzie began in a controlled voice, gathering every ounce of her patience.

"Oh hey, Kenz. You're home already? I must have lost track of time." Raquel came into Kenzie's bedroom wearing Kenzie's towel and dripping water on Kenzie's floor.

"I thought I asked you not to use my room?"

"Oh, but that was the shower. It's not in your room," Raquel said.

Kenzie closed her eyes, praying for more patience than she possessed.

"It's in my bath*room*," Kenzie explained.

"Oh, I guess it is. Cool. I'll take showers in the other bathroom, then," Raquel said with an easy smile, as if it was of no consequence. And it really wouldn't have been, had Raquel not ignored everything else Kenzie had asked of her.

"The house is a mess," Kenzie said, breathing deeply and trying to keep her voice under control.

"I'll clean up the laundry tomorrow," Raquel promised as she walked back into Kenzie's bathroom and pulled out Kenzie's blow dryer.

"Stop using my stuff!" Kenzie screamed.

Raquel slowly set the blow dryer back on the counter, her eyes wide. "Is it a special blow dryer?"

"No. But it's mine. Just like this house is mine. And it would be nice if you respected that instead of treating all of my stuff like crap." Kenzie refrained from shrieking this time, if barely.

"Oh," Raquel said quietly.

"Raquel, I asked you to keep the dogs outside and have the place cleaned up. Bryan is coming over in," Kenzie looked at her watch, "less than an hour."

"Crap. Crap, crap, crap," Raquel muttered as she hopped around the bathroom for who knew what reason. "I thought that was tomorrow."

"I told you last night it was tomorrow," Kenzie said.

"Right, tomorrow."

"No, today. Because yesterday tomorrow was today," Kenzie said.

Raquel eyed her questioningly. She looked a lot like Justin when she did that. The dog, not the singer.

"Today. Less than an hour. Bryan will be here. Bryan who is massively allergic to dogs," Kenzie reiterated.

"Oh, Kenz. I'm so sorry. I'll get it all cleaned up . . . " Raquel began, her voice trailing off as she realized the impossibility.

"I'll text him. We'll just meet up at a restaurant," Kenzie said, trying to keep the disappointment out of her voice. She'd really been looking forward to having Bryan in her home. *Their* home.

"I didn't mean to . . . I'm so sorry, Kenzie," Raquel said.

Kenzie sighed. Raquel always was. Too bad that regret never translated to actual change.

"So, about the bathroom. Were you just mad at me and that's why you said I couldn't use your shower, or do you mean it?" Raquel asked.

"I mean it," Kenzie said through gritted teeth.

She loved her sister. She loved her sister. She loved her sister.

"CONGRATULATIONS ON THE NEW CLIENT," Kenzie said, lifting her glass of seltzer to clink with Bryan's.

Bryan met the gesture with a smile.

Things were going well for them. After a few sessions with a new therapist who wasn't in love with Bryan—okay, maybe the last one hadn't been, but she had definitely sided with Bryan on everything—and getting to the root of Bryan's anger and teaching Kenzie that she'd been taking her husband for granted, they'd decided to begin dating again. It felt a bit silly but was a lot of fun, more than Kenzie had expected.

They took care to invite one another to events or small happenings, breaking their old habit of saying what they were doing and assuming the other would come. Bryan had taken on more of a full-time role in his company again, now that he knew he was healthy enough to do so. Kenzie had learned that marriage wasn't fifty-fifty; it was one hundred percent from both sides. Now that they were both doing their best to give their all, they were much happier with each other—and themselves.

They'd had some hard talks. Bryan had finally vented about what he'd felt Kenzie had done to him, and Kenzie had been appalled with herself. At her reaction, Bryan had realized he should have been more vocal about his frustrations instead of letting them build up. They both had lists of things to work on, but they were both at the same place: they wanted to be together. They were working to rebuild a better version of what they'd lost. And that felt so good.

"I don't know why Merritt was such a tough sell. But it makes the victory that much sweeter," Bryan said, draining his glass.

"I can imagine. Does that mean you'll be traveling? They're based in New York, right?" Kenzie asked.

Bryan nodded, his smile dimming.

"I'll basically be living in New York for about a month. When we started negotiations, I thought that was going to be one of the best parts about this client, but now I'm not looking forward to it at all."

Despite her disappointment about the travel news, Kenzie grinned. Bryan had been negotiating with Merritt for about the same length of time that they'd been in therapy. She liked hearing that the change in what he wanted had coincided with the work they'd put into their marriage.

"But I was thinking," Bryan said slowly, meeting Kenzie's eyes intently. "Maybe after that time in New York I could move home?" He looked at her with a mixture of hope and trepidation.

Kenzie found herself nodding before she even thought about it. She wanted Bryan home more than anything. And it wasn't just because that would allow her to kick out her current roommate.

"In a month?" Kenzie asked, needing a specific timeline. She was already counting down the days.

"Yeah. I'll still have to do a couple of follow-up trips after that, but the majority of my work should be done then," Bryan said. He met her grin with an equally wide smile.

Their server brought their meals, forcing them both to lean back. Kenzie hadn't realized how their bodies had been moving toward one another across the table as they spoke.

"Really?" Kenzie squeaked as the server left. A month ago, she couldn't have imagined they could get to this place in their relationship. But when two people wanted the same thing and put in the work, miracles happened.

Bryan nodded. "I miss you," he breathed.

Kenzie's throat swelled so she couldn't even say the words, she missed him so much. She was thankful he was in her life and they were going on dates again, but she wanted him the way she'd had him before she'd been foolish enough to give him up.

"I wanted to thank you for coming with me to the hospital for Hazel," Kenzie said, tears filling her eyes. She couldn't think about what Hazel was enduring without them.

"Of course. I know I said I resented so many things, but I still want to be there for you. With you." Bryan reached across the table to take her hands.

Kenzie gave a spontaneous, boisterous laugh as emotion surged through her. She really wished they were having this conversation in the privacy of her home instead of a crowded restaurant. But they were together tonight, and she was going to make the most of it.

"I know. But I wanted to make sure I acknowledged and appreciated the way you were there for me. And to let you know I want to be there for you, too."

Bryan nodded. "I know," he replied without any resentment.

Man, they'd come a long way.

"How is Hazel?" Bryan asked, changing the subject before Kenzie could disgrace herself by crying in public.

Kenzie gave him the rundown of what she knew. Hazel was still worn out from her last chemo treatment, but she was trying to stay positive and keep up not only her own spirits but her friends' as well. Basically, she was a rock star.

"And how are things with Raquel?" Bryan asked.

Kenzie's shoulders slumped.

"Can we talk about your new neighbor first?" she hedged, not ready to dredge up all of the contention she felt when talking about her sister. "I've been meaning to ask about him."

Bryan laughed. "You mean Mr. Late Night Serenade?"

Kenzie nodded. Bryan had let her listen to the guy for a minute while they'd been on the phone a couple of nights before. The new next-door neighbor liked to go out onto his porch around eleven each night and sing to the city of San Francisco. Bryan didn't mind because the music never lasted long and he rarely headed to bed before midnight, but other neighbors weren't as accepting.

"So the first serenade was about a week ago, and he's actually got a great voice," Bryan said.

Kenzie nodded. She'd heard him, and he wasn't bad. Not radio worthy, but definitely not nails on a chalkboard either.

"There was a bit of yelling around eleven-thirty, so he stopped singing. But then he went back out that night we were on the phone," Bryan said.

"I remember," Kenzie recalled, carving off a bite of her chicken. They'd been so intent on their conversation she'd almost forgotten to start eating.

"After we got off the phone, I left my patio door open because I had a feeling the entertainment wouldn't stop at just the singing. And I was right. I heard some of the neighbors talking about getting together to sign a petition or something to give to the condo board. So people are not pleased."

Kenzie's eyes went wide. That sounded serious.

"About ten minutes into the singing, I heard a splat."

Kenzie cocked her head.

"Exactly what I thought. Late Night Serenade stopped and then he yelled, 'Who's throwing tomatoes?'"

"No!" Kenzie's mouth opened in shock.

"Right? I thought that would be the end of it but the lady above him started bellowing. I couldn't hear her clearly, but from what I could pick up, the tomato came from her."

"Oh my word," Kenzie breathed.

"Then the guy above me came out, shouting at the woman."

"The woman above Late Night Serenade?" Kenzie clarified.

Bryan nodded, his grin widening.

"He started saying that the condo board was now going to see the tomato as retaliating and it would be that much harder for them to get Late Night Serenade kicked out. Late Night Serenade heard and started getting upset that people were trying to kick him out. Apparently, the condo belongs to his parents, and they'd be ticked to know what he was doing."

"You got more than your ticket price with this show," Kenzie chuckled as Bryan paused to take a bite of his steak.

"And then some. They were all shouting when sirens sounded from below us."

"Someone called the cops?" Kenzie asked.

Bryan nodded but took another bite rather than elaborating.

"And then?" Kenzie prodded.

"I don't know. I closed my door and let the cops handle it."

Kenzie began laughing.

"You can't be nosy for so long and then pull out just when things get good," she reprimanded between giggles.

"I can and I did," Bryan retorted, joining her laughter.

It felt so good to laugh with Bryan like this. She knew they still had many hard times ahead, but these moments were worth fighting for.

"So, Raquel?" Bryan circled back.

Kenzie was pleased he'd remembered, even if she wasn't thrilled to be talking about her sister. But she needed to fill Bryan in, especially since Raquel was the reason they'd had to change their date venue that evening.

Trying to keep her emotions in check, she explained what their house was like and what had happened that day. "Don't worry. I'm already planning on having the place professionally cleaned before you come home. Especially the carpets," Kenzie reassured.

"You don't need to do all that. I'm sure I'll be fine." Bryan tried to put Kenzie at ease.

"Not with this dog hair, you won't. We need it all gone, or you'll be miserable. Although Justin, Mark, and Nick are really cute."

Bryan raised an eyebrow.

"You know how Raquel feels about boybands."

Bryan nodded with a chuckle.

Yup, her sister was one of a kind.

"Will you survive this month?" Bryan asked, worry furrowing his brow.

Kenzie grinned because she knew he'd like her answer. "Knowing you're coming home at the end of it? Yeah, for sure."

Bryan's smile was quick and bright. She hadn't realized how much she'd missed that. His smile used to be like sunshine for her, and it was beginning to feel the same way again.

"Do you think Raquel will be okay with moving out?" he asked.

"She knew the situation was temporary. I think a month will be enough time to help her get on her feet . . . and just short enough that I won't disown or kill her."

"Sounds like it's perfect timing," Bryan said.

Kenzie's grin somehow managed to widen. It sure did.

CHAPTER TEN

"CALLIE, the guests in room ten broke their dresser. They're asking for a replacement." Jenny, the girl working at the front desk, explained. Callie had stopped to check in with her on her way out the door.

"The dresser?" Callie groaned.

She and the staff had anticipated broken light fixtures, perhaps damaged mattresses, and even the need to replace a bed frame now and then, but the dresser? The furniture was just a couple of months old, and sturdily built.

"That's what they told me," Jenny said, shrugging and pointing to the phone she'd just hung up.

Callie took a deep breath. She could do this. It was her job, her livelihood. And the livelihood of many others, including four of the women she loved most in this world.

"How did it break?" Callie asked, wondering if it was neglect on their part or the fault of their guests. She was guessing it was the latter, but they had so few guests right now. She really didn't want to upset the ones they had.

Jenny shrugged again. "The woman on the phone sounded frantic. She didn't really take time to explain anything."

"Frantic about a dresser?" Callie asked, cocking her head in disbelief. She'd seen some strange things since starting this new venture, but this might be toward the top of the list, though she had a feeling it wouldn't stay there long. This job seemed to show her the weirdest side of people.

"Right? I guess they really like having working dressers," Jenny said.

"Okay. Can you get Frank on it?" Callie asked. Since the budget was tight at the moment, they didn't have a full-time handyman, but Frank could typically be there within minutes as long as he wasn't on another job.

Jenny nodded, picking up the phone again.

"Have him look it over. If it's a quick and easy fix—I'm guessing a drawer is off the rail or something—then hopefully he can take care of it. If it looks like more than that, I'm guessing it's the fault of the guests. Maybe that was why the woman was frantic? We'll have to examine it, and if that's the case we'll be charging the card they have on file. We can always bring in a dresser from another room, but if they damage that one too, they'll have to pay for it as well," Callie decided. She really didn't want to charge her guests extra, but if they broke the furniture, it was fair, right?

"Wait, you want me to tell them that?" Jenny asked, her eyes wide.

Callie nodded. It was definitely one of the harder parts of Jenny's job, but considering most of her job consisted of waiting for guests who were few and far between, Callie was sure she could handle it.

"In the most tactful way possible, yeah," Callie said, stepping back so Jenny could start making the calls. Hopefully, Frank could just fix the issue and they could all continue with their day. Happy guest, happy staff, and happy Callie.

"Callie!" called another voice just as she left Jenny's desk. Beth, one of their housekeepers, hurried toward her.

"Yes?" Callie sighed. She had planned to leave more than fifteen minutes ago, and that had already been cutting it close. She'd really wanted some time to get ready for her first date with Leo.

Even with everything on her plate, her stomach flipped at the thought of going out with the man who'd already begun to win her heart. It was crazy how she already felt for him, considering that they'd never even been on an actual date.

She glanced at her watch and frowned. There was no time to dwell on the handsome man who was supposed to be picking her up in forty-three minutes. So much for getting ready in any kind of leisurely manner. If she could get home and change her outfit, maybe touch up her makeup . . .

"Callie!" Sylvia, the other housekeeper, raced down the front steps, trying to catch up to Beth.

Callie was sure she'd talked to the housekeepers about being careful in the public parts of the Lodge, where guests might be passing through. Racing down their main staircase didn't feel careful at all.

"I didn't ask her to clean my rooms. Why should I have to clean hers?" Sylvia said before Beth had a chance to speak.

Callie was lost. Clearly she was coming in on the middle of a conversation.

"I read your text wrong, and I cleaned rooms ten to twenty," Beth explained.

Callie really wanted to hire someone to oversee housekeeping, but right now they couldn't afford it, so she was stuck with the job. Every morning she texted the housekeepers their assignments, along with making sure the handyman was called for repairs, helping Saffron oversee the kitchen staff, trying to fill the rooms with Laurel, making sure finances weren't too far off the rails with Kenzie, and taking over all of the customer service stuff Hazel had planned to be in charge of.

Hazel.

But Callie had no time to dwell on her friend. Kenzie would be going over tonight to keep Hazel company, and Hazel had told Callie that the best thing she could do for her was to enjoy her date with Leo.

Heavens, she needed to focus on the task at hand. She felt like she was losing her ever-loving mind. There was always tragedy just around the corner, and Callie was tired of putting out a fire just to have another flare up moments later. There was only so much of her and her time, and she was spread too thin.

But there was no time to complain about that either, even in her own head. She had to focus on her housekeepers.

"Beth, you were supposed to clean ten to fifteen and then twenty-one through twenty-five." Callie had memorized the schedule she'd implemented. With the Lodge far from full, empty rooms were cleaned every few days, while the occupied rooms were cleaned every morning. Beth, who worked the dayshift, was supposed to clean those occupied rooms, and Sylvia cleaned the empty rooms on rotation each evening when she came in.

Callie slipped out her phone and double-checked to make sure she'd texted correctly. Thank heavens, she had.

"I know that now, but I cleaned sixteen to twenty already," Beth explained. "It's not fair that I have to clean twenty-one to twenty-five as well."

"But those rooms are occupied," Sylvia protested. "They'll take twice as long. If I clean all of those, even starting right now, I won't get to twenty-five until about nine P.M. I doubt guests will be pleased at their room being cleaned so late in the evening."

"Beth, it really is your fault. You should have read my

text more carefully," Callie said, trying to sound diplomatic even though she really just felt frustrated. How hard was it to read a text? She turned toward the check-in desk.

"Jenny, which rooms between twenty-one and twenty-five are occupied for tonight?" she asked, hoping some were empty and wouldn't need immediate cleaning.

"Twenty-one and twenty-two. We have a family checking in late this evening and were planning to put them in twenty-four, though," Jenny said as she looked over the bookings on their computer.

"Since Beth already cleaned sixteen, put the new guests in there," Callie decided.

Jenny nodded, and Callie turned her attention back to her housekeepers.

"Twenty-one and twenty-two are the immediate priority. It's Beth's responsibility, but since time is short, I want Beth to clean twenty-one and Sylvia to do twenty-two. After that, Beth, you can finish the rest of your assignment. I'm sorry if that keeps you here late, but it's not fair to give Sylvia your work."

Callie felt that was fair, although neither employee seemed particularly pleased. But she needed them to pay attention to directions and then do their jobs without constant supervision. Callie really did appreciate both of her housekeepers. She just didn't have the time to micromanage their tasks.

Callie sighed yet again. Whoever said that being the boss was a good gig had lied.

Jenny sent her a commiserating look as if she understood just how hard the last thirty minutes had been on Callie.

Thirty minutes?!

She looked at her watch and saw that it was indeed just half an hour from the time Leo was picking her up.

She groaned. It would take her ten minutes to get home—if

the traffic lights were in her favor—so that really gave her just twenty minutes to get ready. That was enough time for an outfit change and makeup touch-up, right?

If she got out the door right now. She began speed walking.

"What are you still doing here, Call?" Laurel asked as she walked out from her office behind the front desk.

Callie shrugged, slowing but not stopping. She didn't have time to explain everything.

"Well, get out of here," Laurel directed, making a shooing motion with her hands.

Callie hurried toward the entrance. She was almost out the door when Jimmy, a waiter at the restaurant, stopped her.

"Do you mind asking Saffron if I can get next weekend off?" he asked Callie, then turned around as if the job was done. He'd asked a question, but it had really been a demand.

"Jimmy, ask Saffron yourself. Callie is off for the night," Laurel said from where she stood beside Jenny, watching the exchange.

"Callie's already going home?" Jimmy asked.

It was a fair question. When was the last time she'd left work before ten P.M.? The Lodge had become her life.

"Yes, she is. So go find Saffron on your own," Laurel ordered, waving Callie off once more.

Callie was grateful for Laurel's interference, but she'd lost another few minutes of her very limited time.

She wasn't going to let it get to her. Tonight would be nice even if she didn't have a chance to get ready the way she wanted to. It didn't matter.

As she got into her car and drove away, Callie kept repeating that to herself. Life was not going the way she'd imagined it, but Hazel was the one with the short end of the stick right now, not Callie. So what if it meant a little more work for her? It was nothing compared to what her friend was enduring. Callie had no room to complain.

And yet she found it hard to breathe. She just needed a day off, maybe two. But since the Lodge had opened, none of them had gotten a full day off. They took shifts, at least one of them at the Lodge at all times. More often than not, Callie was that person. Laurel had her kids, Kenzie was working things out with her husband, and even Saffron had family responsibilities. Callie's family was used to her working twenty-four-seven and had come to expect little from her.

Pulling up to the third red light in a row, Callie felt tears begin streaming down her cheeks. This was stupid. Why was she crying?

All she'd wanted was a little time to get ready for a date she'd looked forward to for months. She'd hoped Leo would ask her out from the first moment he'd handed her a sugar-filled coffee, and now it was happening. But it was all wrong. She was supposed to be home in time to get ready at her leisure, maybe even take a bath before picking the perfect outfit and making sure she looked her best.

Looking at the time now and the next red light in front of her, she'd be lucky to have time to apply deodorant, brush her teeth, and put on some lipstick.

That was all she would get to do before meeting a man who would look equal parts gorgeous and dashing. Callie knew she was just mediocre in the looks department, but she wanted to at least feel her best for a man she liked so much.

But she wasn't going to get that.

And if tears kept falling down her cheeks, she was going to look like a raccoon. She could practically feel the mascara smudging under her eyes.

"Buck up, Callie," she muttered to herself as she finally pulled into her driveway.

Where another car was already parked.

Leo. He was early. She should have been thrilled that he was so eager to see her that he came early.

But as she pulled past him into the garage and put her car into park, the waterworks really started and there was no way to stop them.

She was a fool. A foolish, spoiled woman who didn't deserve to go out on a date with this man. Because a few things had gone wrong, she was pouting like a toddler instead of just being thankful this date was happening. It was beyond her wildest dreams. So what if it wasn't happening in a perfect manner? So what if her employees were all mad at her? So what if she worked so many hours she should just call the Lodge home these days? So what if she was so tired that her eyes were always red and veiny? They were doubtless even worse now that she was sobbing.

She was a mess.

A knock sounded at her window. Leo was here.

She closed her eyes. He should run the other direction. She didn't want him to see her like this, and yet, she couldn't very well ignore him. He was right there.

He probably *should* see her like this. He should know that he was so much better than she was, if he didn't already.

Callie sighed as she opened her door. Tears still streamed down her cheeks, defying her efforts to stop the flow.

"Callie," Leo whispered. Gently he pulled her out of the car and into his arms.

The torrent of tears had no reason to subside. She was being comforted by the kindest soul and strongest shoulder she knew. She breathed in the scent of his spicy cologne and the faint smell of wood. It smelled so good. Leo smelled so good.

Focusing on the fact that it was Leo holding her and her

tears were wetting his shirt, Callie finally managed to stop crying and pulled away. Leo hadn't signed on for any of this.

She waited for him to let her go. Any other man she'd dated would have been gone long before this.

But he still held her close.

"Are you just now getting home from the Lodge?" he asked.

Callie sniffled and nodded.

"You went in early today, right?"

She nodded again. She'd texted Leo her plans that morning. She'd had grand designs of going in at six so that she could leave by five for their date. It was a bit strange that they were everyday texters before their first date, but they had been coworkers, then friends. Callie had hoped for more tonight, but it looked like she'd ruined that.

She'd been so excited. Now look at her.

"Rough day?" he asked, trying to meet her shifting eyes. But the last thing she wanted was for Leo to gaze into her red, swollen eyes.

"It's just a lot, you know?" Callie's voice broke. She shouldn't be complaining. Her life was so good . . . other than the fact that her best friend had cancer and her personal life always took a back seat to work and she was so danged tired.

"I know," Leo said, pulling Callie even closer so she had to lean her head on his shoulder.

Just as she'd been doing figuratively for the past couple of months. Leo had become her sounding board. She didn't feel she could complain about the Lodge to her friends, not when work affected them as much as her. Nor her worry for Hazel. She didn't want to add to her friends' plates. So Leo had been a listening third party who'd been ready to hear all of her worries and fears, and often eased them with his nightly texts.

"How about this? I cancel our reservation," Leo said, still holding her close.

Callie's heart dropped. He was leaving her. As he should. She'd already put so much on him, and this was the last straw. She looked a mess, she felt a mess, and she was sure she even smelled a mess.

Callie nodded, feeling tears resurge. But she'd hold them back until Leo left. She didn't want him to stay out of guilt. He was too good of a man to leave her if he thought he was hurting her. She was sure he was doing this for her—giving her the night off that she looked like she needed.

But she didn't need it. Well, maybe she *did* need it, but she wanted it with Leo.

"And I'll get us some takeout. You go and take a bath or do whatever you want to relax, and I'll be in the living room waiting. You have ESPN, right?" he asked.

Callie giggled in relief and pure exhilaration. He wasn't leaving her. She was going to get what she needed and wanted. How had she managed to find a man who not only planned romantic dates but could sense her needs and instantly change his plans to meet those needs?

"You're giving me a chill night at home with you?" Callie asked, still incredulous at his suggestion.

He wasn't leaving her alone. What man did this?

"As long as you want me. I don't want to intrude," he said, looking like he was worried he'd overstepped.

"I do want you," Callie said immediately. She wanted Leo beside her, but it was more than just a craving for a handsome man now. She was beginning to need all parts of Leo.

"Then it's settled," Leo said, taking her hand and leading her through her garage door toward the house.

It was. And suddenly Callie felt lighter than she had in a long time. She no longer felt alone.

CHAPTER ELEVEN

"IT LOOKS like Call and Leo have opted for a night in," Laurel said as she and Saffron walked out to their cars that evening after Saffron had closed the kitchen. Jenny was in charge of the front desk for the night, so Saffron and Laurel had been able to leave at a decent hour. That was one nice thing about only serving lunch. Saffron often got home by six or seven P.M. instead of the wee hours of the morning.

"Nice," Saffron said, grinning. That sounded like a date right up Callie's alley. She thanked every lucky star that Callie had found a man who seemed to understand and care about her. Saffron had great hopes for Callie and Leo.

"But I'm guessing that means you'll want a place to hide out tonight?" Saffron added, remembering that Laurel shared a home with Callie for the time being.

Laurel nodded. "I really need to get my own place. But with things at the Lodge being so up in the air financially, it doesn't seem like the smartest time to sign a lease."

Saffron nodded in understanding.

"Do you want to come to my house?" Saffron asked. "I'm

supposed to go over to the Grangers for a bit, but I can give you the key."

"That would actually be fantastic. I was going to ask one of my kids if I could come over, but the idea of that drive right now . . ." Laurel cringed.

"Here ya go." Saffron handed Laurel her house key. "I should be back by nine. Mrs. Granger goes to bed pretty early."

"But does Alex?" Laurel asked cheekily.

Saffron paused to look at her friend as they both reached their cars.

"No, but I'm going over to see his mother, not him." Saffron stated the obvious. Ever since she'd helped care for Mrs. Granger when Alex was out of town, Saffron had made an effort to see her at least once a week. It gave Alex an evening off if he needed it, and she truly enjoyed Mrs. Granger's company.

"Right," Laurel teased.

"You keep that up and I'm taking my key back. How does a long drive into the city sound?" Saffron teased right back.

"Alright, I'm sorry," Laurel said meekly as she got into her car, but then added, "kind of!" just before she shut the door.

"Punk," Saffron muttered as she got into her own car, watching Laurel laugh and drive away.

The drive to the Grangers didn't take long. Saffron had only made it a few times, but it already felt like a natural route, and she wasn't sure what to make of that. Sure, she and Mrs. Granger had become friends, but was her draw to the house more than that, as Laurel had implied?

No, Laurel was just messing with her. Saffron and Alex were friends. She and Mrs. Granger were friends. That was it—no more, no less. And it was all Saffron wanted. Even if she couldn't help replaying the conversation when Mrs. Granger had admitted that her son had had a crush on Saffron back in high school. But high school was so very long ago. And there was no way Alex could feel the same way now. He'd practically dragged her into the friend zone and then erected a fence, keeping Saffron firmly in place outside his heart. Besides, Saffron didn't want Alex to feel the same way he had back then, did she? No, the friend zone was good for them. Especially since Alex didn't see marriage in his future.

Saffron parked along the street, taking in the vibrant green yard and the well-trimmed oak trees on either side of the driveway. Alex had found a beautiful place to call home, and he was the best kind of son to share it with his mom in her time of need.

Saffron noticed that the garage door was open and Alex's typical spot was empty. Aja's car sat in the driveway, but it felt strange that Alex was gone. Sure, he hadn't been here the first couple of times when Saffron had come over while he was at the wedding, but he'd made sure to be home the ensuing two evenings she'd come to visit Mrs. Granger.

Saffron reminded herself that she had insisted Alex take some time to himself these evenings she visited. That must be what he was doing, and she was glad for him. He'd worked from six until two that day, taking over prep in the morning so Saffron could sleep in a bit, and he deserved some time to just unwind.

Saffron walked up to the house and rapped softly on the door. She never knew when Mrs. Granger could be sleeping and didn't want to disturb her if she was.

"Come in," Aja called.

Saffron guessed Mrs. Granger wasn't napping.

She walked in and took off her shoes by the door. She hadn't realized the Grangers were a shoe-free household the first time she'd visited, but she liked that custom. There was something homey about taking one's shoes off, and it made Saffron feel immediately comfortable.

She glanced to her left and saw Aja working in the kitchen. She often prepped Mrs. Granger's meals the evening before so the next day could go more smoothly. From where she stood, Saffron could see the back of Mrs. Granger's head against the couch in the living room as her favorite show filled the TV screen.

"What is Haleakala," Mrs. Granger answered with the contestant.

"Hey, Mrs. Granger!" Saffron said brightly as she entered the living room.

"Hello, Saffron!" Mrs. Granger replied, matching Saffron's energy.

Saffron grinned broadly. Mrs. Granger remembered her. It must be a good day.

"You can head out whenever you're ready," Saffron said to Aja, who nodded.

"I'll just finish up this meal prep and then I will. Thanks," Aja said as she turned back to her work.

"So what are the plans for tonight?" Saffron asked, turning her full attention back to Mrs. Granger.

"I was planning on watching my show until you interrupted that," Mrs. Granger teased lightheartedly, nodding toward her TV.

Saffron chuckled.

"We could do that," Saffron said, taking a seat on the couch next to Mrs. Granger.

"Nah, I do that all the time. How about a card game?" Mrs. Granger asked, clicking off the TV with the remote.

"Love to," Saffron responded, and before she could stand up to search for the cards, Aja handed them to her.

Aja had her purse on her shoulder. She must be headed out.

"Have a good night," Saffron called as Aja headed toward the front door.

Watching Aja leave reminded Saffron of who wasn't there. She didn't *need* to know where Alex was, but she had to admit she was a bit curious. But then again, Alex would have to come home before she could leave, so she'd have a chance to ask him.

"So what's the game, Mrs. Granger?" Saffron asked as she set up a folding TV tray between herself and the other lady.

Mrs. Granger pursed her lips thoughtfully. "How about you call me Paula?" she said, catching Saffron by surprise. She had been ready for the name of a card game. But she liked the request. It would be nice to call Mrs. Granger by her first name.

"Sounds good to me," Saffron said happily.

"And let's play Trash," Paula added.

"Trash?" Saffron raised a skeptical eyebrow.

"I used to play it with Alex all the time when he was a kid."

Saffron tried to keep her grin from growing too wide. She liked the idea of glimpsing Alex's past.

Paula explained the simple rules, and while Saffron could see how a child would enjoy it, she found herself loving it too. The game quickly became competitive.

"Down four games to two. It's a little bit sad, don't you think?" Paula crowed.

Saffron laughed. They'd been trash talking good-naturedly from the beginning of the game. One thing she and Paula had in common: they liked to win.

"Yeah, yeah. But who's been playing this game for years? It's my first night," Saffron reminded her.

"The rules aren't that tough," Paula swung back.

"There's still something to be said for experience."

Paula didn't argue with that as she dealt another hand.

The sound of a door opening and closing caused the women to look up. Smiles covered both of their faces as Alex joined them.

"Is my mom cheating?" Alex asked.

Saffron's mouth dropped open and Paula exclaimed, "I never cheat! Alex is just sore that he can never beat me."

"That may be true. But I don't ever have a hard time beating other people—just you, Mom," Alex countered.

"I'm just better at cards than all of your friends. Not my fault." Paula shrugged her dainty shoulders.

This woman was the best.

"Are you losing?" Alex asked Saffron.

She nodded.

"See, now I'm convinced. Saffron is amazing at anything she does," Alex argued.

It took everything in Saffron not to turn to mush at the compliment.

"Everything except for cards, evidently," Paula answered too quickly, causing all three of them to laugh.

"So how was your date?" Paula asked her son as the laughter died down.

Date?

All of Saffron's giddiness fled. Alex had been on a date. Of course he had. He was a handsome, charming, and very single man. Why wouldn't he date when given a night off from caring for his mother? He *should* go on a date.

"Good." Alex went to the fridge and opened it, pulling out a jug of orange juice. He drank straight from the container, and typically, Saffron would have been grossed out, but watching Alex's Adam's apple bob as he drank . . . well, her thoughts strayed a bit.

Dang the man and his date! His "good" date no less.

Saffron had been fine with being friend zoned. It felt like the right place for her. Until she realized he wasn't out there friend-zoning everyone. Just her. And now she couldn't help asking *why*. What was it about *her*?

"Can you handle one more game of Trash?" Paula asked, and Saffron wanted to say yes. She was going to say yes until Paula added, "And while we play, Alex can tell us all about his date with Viola."

That made Saffron's decision for her.

"I think I'd better go," she said, standing and faking a regretful smile. "My friend Laurel is at my place this evening, and I've left her alone for long enough."

"Oh, I didn't realize that. You should have brought her along," Paula said, reminding Saffron why she was there. Not for the handsome man now replacing the juice in the fridge, but for his kind mother who'd seemed like she could use another friend.

"Next time I will. But thanks for the great night, Paula. I needed it."

Despite how she felt about Alex dating Viola, what Saffron told her new friend was the truth. It had been a wonderful evening, and it had helped to ease some of the stress that had been building up recently. Hazel's cancer, the Lodge's financial issues, the fact that the restaurant was mostly empty—all of it was slowly eating away at Saffron. But she'd been able to ignore it for most of the night, and for that, she felt so much gratitude.

"Me too, sweetie," Paula said as she patted Saffron's cheek.

Saffron grinned as she stood and headed toward the front door.

"Let me walk you out," Alex said, following her.

Her heart leapt, but she told it to stay down where it belonged. No leaping for Alex, the man dating Viola.

Saffron didn't answer verbally, but she did slow down so they could walk side by side once they were out the door.

"I don't think I can thank you enough for what you've been for my mom, for how much you've helped me," Alex said, his words so full of gratitude that Saffron had to accept them. Some of the hard feelings that had begun building up about Viola and about herself being stuck in the friend zone started dissipating.

"Of course. I wanted to help, but now I feel like I'm getting the better end of the deal. Spending time with Paula is a treat."

They paused by Saffron's car, and Alex studied her. She wasn't sure what he was looking for, but it made her anxious, so she moved around the car to open her door.

"See you tomorrow," she said, eager to get out of there before she did anything stupid. Like tell Alex how nice he looked in his green-collared shirt and fitting-just-right jeans or ask who the heck Viola was.

She pressed her lips shut and closed the door behind her.

But even with the walls of the car separating them, Saffron still felt that pesky pull toward Alex. The one she'd been disregarding since he'd walked back into her life a couple of months before. It should have been easy, considering he was dating someone else. And that he'd put her in the friend zone long before that. They were right where they ought to be—he worked for her, for heaven's sake. She was being an idiot.

So Saffron started her car and ignored the way Alex continued to watch her. She ignored the small smile on his lips, and she even ignored the way his hand went to her passenger's door as if reaching for the handle.

She just couldn't ignore that she really wished she had been the one to go out with Alex that evening.

That decided it. As soon as she got home, she would ask Laurel to help her with an online dating profile. Saffron had been on dating sites many times before, but had taken a break after moving back to Rosebud. Now the time was right. She needed to get back out there. She was feeling melancholy about Alex only because there was no one else in her life. So she'd meet more men, go on fantastic dates, and she'd be fine. Great, even.

With that, Saffron drove away.

LAUREL SAT in the corner of her parents' living room, smiling at anyone who looked her way. She was playing a precarious role that evening. Her parents were holding their first gathering since everything with Bennie had been revealed, and they'd insisted on inviting Laurel, even though she knew it was only because of her association with Bennie that her parents had ever stopped holding their much-anticipated parties. So Laurel was present, doing her best to look supportive and happy for her parents but trying to stay as unobtrusive as possible. No need to remind the partygoers of why the parties had stopped.

After the mess with Bennie, her parents had laid low for a while, even though they had been his victims as well. They'd invested a good chunk of their retirement with him, but many of the other victims had still found reason to be upset with Laurel's mom and dad.

And for that, Laurel wasn't sure she could ever forgive Bennie. Not that she had any sort of communication with her ex at the moment. She'd have to deal with their relationship some-day. But for now it was enough that her parents and children could move on with their lives.

Laurel heard her mother laugh and had to smile. She was glad things had returned to normal for them and that they'd been so willing to forgive even those who'd turned on them. Laurel's mother had explained that people had been hurting, and when people are hurt they lash out. So it was up to Laurel's parents to decide: did they want to throw away decades-long friendships because of things said in moments of weakness? They'd both decided they didn't, and that decision seemed to be working for them. They seemed truly happy and secure in their lives again. For that Laurel was grateful, even if her own life was still so up in the air.

"I've heard wonderful things about the Lodge," said Mrs. Chu, next-door neighbor to Laurel's parents, as she took a seat on the couch next to Laurel.

Laurel grinned, feeling like her mouth was stretching a bit too much, but fake smiles could do that. It was hard to take compliments about the Lodge when it was struggling. But she and her friends had decided to keep quiet about their reservations all but drying up. First of all, they didn't want to worry the town, and second, if whoever was sabotaging them lived in town, which seemed likely, they didn't want that person or people to feel like they'd won. So for now, they were keeping any and all bad news just between themselves. Laurel was sure some of the employees could see for themselves that business wasn't great, but the girls worked hard to appear upbeat in front of their workers.

"The grand opening seemed like it was quite the success. It was a beautiful event," Mrs. Chu continued.

It had been. This time Laurel's smile was genuine. She was proud of the event they'd put on. She'd almost forgotten Mrs. Chu had been on the guest list. They'd invited so many people it was hard to remember who had been there. But since Mr. Chu was on the city council, it had made sense to invite them.

"Thank you," Laurel said. "The girls all worked hard."

"And you did as well. I didn't miss the way you were running around the entire evening." Mrs. Chu patted Laurel's leg.

"I'm just thankful I get to work with my best friends," Laurel said.

Mrs. Chu smiled softly. "That's so nice for you. Especially after these past few months." She leaned in as if she was going to tell Laurel a secret. "I just want you to know that I don't blame you or your parents for what happened with Bennie."

Laurel felt her throat clog with emotion. She hadn't forgotten. Mr. and Mrs. Chu had been victims of Bennie's scam, investing at the same time Laurel's parents had.

"I'm so sorry," Laurel began, but Mrs. Chu hushed her.

"You've said that plenty these past months, and although I wasn't quite receptive to it at first, I now see what a terrible friend I've been to all of you. I was just so scared. All of our retirement was tied up in Bennie's scheme."

Laurel nodded, wincing as she remembered how hard the Chus had been hit.

"But we're moving forward. Thankfully Mr. Chu is still working, and we had a few investments that weren't associated with Bennie, and I'm sure it will all work out. I'm still fearful at times, but I've been able to see past that and know that the three of you deserved none of my ire," Mrs. Chu continued as she looked from Laurel to her parents.

Laurel felt tears fall down her cheeks. She was so thankful to be forgiven, and she still didn't feel like she deserved it.

"Hey, no tears. I've cried enough for all of us," Mrs. Chu joked.

Laurel let out a choked laugh.

"We really haven't been fair to you—all of us. We were over at the Fields' the other night, and they were saying the same thing."

Oh, the Fields. They'd been another family hit hard by Bennie. Laurel's stomach sank. She'd been able to give some money to the victims hit the very hardest, but now that the Lodge was struggling, Laurel had to hold onto what was left of her meager savings, the little that hadn't been touched by the government.

When she ran out of available funds, there was a long list of people she hadn't been able to help. The Fields probably would have been next on the list as far as people who needed the money the most. They had six kids, and although they both had good jobs, all of their savings had been tied up with Bennie. Laurel had cried many tears when she'd heard some of those savings were for their kids' college funds. Now they were living paycheck to paycheck, starting over. And they had a daughter ready to start college that very next year.

"Don't look like that, Laurel. I see it written all over your face. I'm bringing this up to say we don't blame you. The Fields were lamenting poor Hazel's diagnosis; their son is friends with Sterling."

Oh, that was right.

"So they were just saying that you poor women have been hit too hard, between what Bennie did to you and now Hazel."

Laurel didn't have anything to say to that. If only Mrs. Chu knew that was just the tip of the iceberg the Rosebud Girls were facing.

"Though they were still plenty angry with Bennie, especially Lisha."

"She's their oldest, right?" Laurel asked.

Mrs. Chu nodded. "She was headed to MIT, but now they aren't sure if they can handle the costs. They've considered loans, but they're not sure they should go into so much debt."

Laurel's stomach tightened. The poor girl.

"Actually, you might want to talk to her if you get the chance. She's angry with the whole world about this mess. Bennie especially, but she also said it wasn't fair that you get to move on with your new job while the rest of our lives are obliterated. Her parents laughed at her, calling it teenaged drama, but I couldn't help but feel there was some threat behind what she said. She's a smart girl. Smart and angry aren't the greatest combination."

Laurel was about to wave away Mrs. Chu's concerns but suddenly froze as an idea hit her.

That's what had felt so wrong about all of this. A social

media smear campaign wasn't like adult revenge. It was the kind of thing that happened in high school. The actions of a teenager. A very angry, extremely tech-savvy teenager.

But, no. Laurel couldn't blame this on Lisha Fields. The poor girl was already about to lose her whole future. She couldn't risk being wrong.

But what if it was Lisha, and Laurel ignored it, causing the Lodge to go under? She'd have missed her chance to save the livelihoods of her four best friends and all of their employees.

Her stomach twisted so hard she felt a roil of nausea.

"Are you okay, sweetheart?" Mrs. Chu asked, looking at her in concern.

Laurel nodded. "It was lovely speaking with you, but I just realized I forgot to do something at work." She stood.

"You work too hard," Mrs. Chu said with a smile, oblivious to the fact that her information had sent Laurel into a tailspin.

Could a kid have done all of this?

The more Laurel thought about it, the more it made sense. But what next? She couldn't very well go to Lisha and ask her. It didn't seem fair to go to her parents, either. Besides, if Lisha was doing this, it was all Laurel's fault. Lisha wouldn't be going after the Lodge if not for what Bennie had cost her family.

But Laurel still returned to her original conclusion. She couldn't allow her friends to suffer for Bennie's actions.

She thought about going to Callie and letting her decide what to do, but that wasn't the right move either. Laurel was an adult. She could do this as well as Callie.

And she needed to do it right now.

Laurel sent a quick goodbye her parents' way and slipped out before either could question why she was leaving. She drove the short distance to the Fields', parking just beside the curb in front of their home.

Bikes were strewn across the front lawn, reminding Laurel

that this was a family home. Kids, younger than her own babies, lived here. And she was about to accuse one of them of a crime.

What was she doing? Laurel had been all keyed up at the possibility of finally getting answers and had driven here without thinking things through. She'd thought she couldn't accuse Lisha, and yet here she sat. What was she planning on doing, if not leveling accusations?

She couldn't do it. At least not without solid proof.

But she'd been searching for proof for weeks, and this was all she had. She didn't have the technological savvy to backtrack any of this stuff. She and Callie had been about to hire Riley's guy to dig into things, but the cost had been astronomical, and the girls had decided to give Laurel a little more time to research before spending that kind of cash. Cash the Lodge couldn't afford unless it was the only way to save it.

So Laurel had to talk to Lisha. She wouldn't accuse her but would ask her . . . what? Laurel felt as if her thoughts were in a spiral. She needed to figure this out for the sake of the friends she loved.

But what if she was wrong?

Laurel couldn't get past that. She and Bennie had already put this family through so much. In her gut, Laurel felt sure Lisha was the culprit; it just made sense. But she couldn't go up to their door just on her gut.

This was all wrong. Hiring Riley's guy was the only solution. Somehow she'd figure out a way to get the money and they'd let him follow the evidence. If it came back to Lisha after that, then Laurel would have this conversation, but not until she had indisputable proof. She couldn't accuse a seventeen-year-old on a gut feeling.

A knock sounded at her window. Laurel jumped and her turbulent thoughts scattered as she looked up, startled.

Alice Fields stood at Laurel's car door with a welcoming grin on her face.

Laurel tried to school her surprised features and rolled down the window.

"Hi, Laurel," Alice said brightly. "We saw you parked here and thought you might need something." Alice pointed to her husband, who was waving from their driveway, standing next to their minivan of escaping children.

Laurel couldn't help but notice the glare their oldest sent her way.

Wait, the whole family had come home? How had Laurel missed them driving right past her and parking? Her thoughts had preoccupied her more than she'd realized.

And now, Laurel was here, in front of Alice. But what was she supposed to say? She'd been about to leave, but now they'd seen her. So what reason could she give for being there?

Her heart beat faster as she tried to come up with a lie. But she came up empty.

So she said the only thing that came to mind. "I had a question for you folks, but I realized I'm okay without the answer." She gave Alice what she hoped was a kind look. Right now, she felt a combination of confused and fearful, so *kind* was a little hard to pull off.

"That's very . . . vague," Alice commented as her husband, Hank, joined her at Laurel's car.

"Hello, Laurel," he said.

Laurel returned the greeting, itching to escape. But then she did think of something better to say.

"And I wanted to apologize for Bennie again."

"Laurel, you've already said sorry more than you should have. Bennie—I'd accept an apology from him. But you, you already gave us one, even though there is no need for you to feel badly. You did nothing wrong," Alice said graciously, although Laurel didn't feel worthy of it.

A scornful mutter sounded behind the Fields.

"Lisha?" Alice asked, turning to look at her oldest.

"What's she doing here?" Lisha practically growled, her eyes narrowed at Laurel.

Mrs. Chu wasn't wrong. The girl was angry with Laurel—bitterness emanated off of her. Not that Laurel blamed her.

"Lisha!" Alice reprimanded as Hank raised his eyebrows at his daughter.

"That's no way to speak to a guest," Hank said sternly.

"Since when did we start calling criminals guests?" Lisha replied.

Alice's head snapped back as if she'd been slapped. "Lisha Fields, you go in the house this instant!" Her voice jumped to a screech.

"Sure, as soon as the trash leaves," Lisha said defiantly, crossing her arms over her chest and glaring at Laurel, leaving no doubt as to who she thought the trash was.

Hank's face turned a shade of red that seemed unhealthy.

"I think that's my cue to leave. But again, I really am sorry," Laurel said as she took off her emergency brake, waiting to put her car into drive until the Fields stepped back. Hank and Alice still stood close to the car, and even in her distracted state Laurel appreciated the evidence of trust and forgiveness.

"No, you have no reason to be sorry, as I said before. But our daughter sure does. Apologize this minute," Alice said, turning to her daughter.

Lisha pursed her lips in response.

"Lisha Fields, say that you're sorry," Hank added.

"I won't lie. Not like her husband," Lisha said, jutting her chin toward Laurel.

"It really isn't necessary," Laurel said, feeling that she'd made a mess of things. If she hadn't come here, none of this would have happened. She didn't blame Lisha for her anger. And now, the teenager was in trouble for things she never would have said had Laurel not shown up.

"Yes, it is," Hank said.

Alice added, speaking to Laurel, "Well, now, the least we can do is answer that question for you."

"What question?" Hank asked.

"Not a big deal. I don't need the answer," Laurel said quickly, trying to deflect so they'd let her drive away. She didn't want Lisha to say anything more—for the girl's sake, not Laurel's.

"Before, you said you were okay without the answer. That doesn't sound like you don't need it. It just sounds like you'll manage. We'd like to at least try to answer your question," Alice said.

"It's the least we can do," Hank added, glancing back at his still fuming daughter.

Laurel swallowed as she looked from the concerned faces of Mr. and Mrs. Fields to the pure fury coming from Lisha.

"I really should go," she tried again. She wouldn't accuse this girl.

But the Fields made no move, so Laurel couldn't leave.

"Please," Hank said, putting a hand on the car as he leaned closer. "If we can help you in some way, we'd love to. We feel terrible that we were ever angry with you over what Bennie did to us. We've talked about it, and if the situation was reversed, we know you would never have treated Alice the way we treated you. You would have seen from the get-go what we know now: it was never your fault. You were maybe the biggest victim of all. And yet you've done nothing but apologize. We heard how you helped the Hernandez family and others. And now our daughter treats you like this? Please, just ask your question," Hank urged.

They weren't going to let her leave. But Laurel couldn't say what she'd been planning. Suddenly, a thought came to her—maybe the only thing that could save her.

"My question was actually for Lisha," Laurel said, trying to smile even as Lisha's continuous glare made her want to wither. She'd leave as soon as she did this.

"And she'll be pleased to answer it," Alice answered for her daughter.

Lisha grunted, but at least she was listening.

"We've been having some issues with negative social media campaigns," Laurel said, trying to keep from accusing Lisha but also asking a question that might help them with the information they needed. "It's been causing us to lose some reservations at the Lodge."

"That's terrible," Alice gasped.

Laurel nodded. "If it just concerned me, I wouldn't have even come here. But I'm worried because my four best friends are counting on this venture to work."

"So these campaigns are hurting your business?" Lisha asked, the first sign of a smile on her face as she took a step toward Laurel's car.

Okay, that didn't mean anything. Lisha was livid with Laurel, clearly. Just because she was pleased with the results of the smear campaign didn't mean she'd done it.

"They are. Mine, Saffron's, Callie's, Kenzie's, and *Hazel's*," Laurel said, emphasizing the last name. If Sterling was friends with Lisha's brother, she would at least feel badly for them, wouldn't she?

But she didn't stop smiling.

"I'm so sorry," Alice said. Then she added, "What was your question for Lisha?"

"Something about the campaigns hit me today. They seem quite juvenile. Not the technique behind them, but the idea of using social media to bring us down."

"Like something a high school bully would do," Hank interjected, nodding in understanding.

"Not a bully if whoever is doing this was hit first," Lisha spouted.

Both parents turned to their daughter. "Why would you say that, Lisha?" Alice asked, raising a questioning eyebrow.

The smile had disappeared from Lisha's face.

"It isn't fair to call this person a bully. I just think they probably have their reasons," Lisha replied. She tried for a nonchalant shrug, but the blood had drained from her face.

"I was just wondering if Lisha knew of anyone capable of this kind of tech savvy, considering she's so smart and goes to Rosebud High," Laurel said, trying to take the heat off the girl. She could still be innocent, and Laurel wasn't going to let her take any blame until it was proved without a doubt.

"I know a girl," Hank said, looking at Lisha.

"Please tell me you didn't do this." Alice's eyes were wide as she took in her daughter's face, now looking more guilty and fearful than angry and defiant.

"I'm not accusing Lisha," Laurel said desperately. This had gone so wrong.

Alice shook her head. "No one is. But I'm asking my daughter a question and I need an immediate answer."

"Of course I didn't," Lisha said quickly. Maybe too quickly. "It's not just kids who use social media, anyway. Especially Facebook. Only old people use Facebook."

"Laurel didn't mention which social media platform was used," Hank said as Alice's eyes filled with tears.

"Where were these campaigns?" Alice turned to Laurel as her tears began to slide down her face.

Laurel hesitated for an agonizing moment, trying to think of a way to soften the blow. "Facebook," she finally admitted in a whisper.

"It was a guess," Lisha said quickly.

"A good guess." Hank's eyes hadn't left his daughter, and his voice was heavy with disappointment.

"Too good," Alice said, swiping at her tears and turning back to Laurel. "How bad is it? Don't sugarcoat it."

"We've lost most of our reservations," Laurel said softly, trying to respect Alice even as her heart broke for Lisha. They all knew Lisha was guilty even if she hadn't yet admitted it.

Laurel had envisioned this going down so differently. When they found their culprit, she expected to feel vindication. She'd finally be able to direct her frustration at someone. But now, seeing that the person behind the campaigns was a child who'd been hurt by Bennie, she felt no joy, no satisfaction. This was absolutely terrible. Tears came to her eyes as well.

Alice nodded. "I didn't think you'd be here unless it was dire. You knew it was Lisha, didn't you?"

Laurel shook her head, thankful she could deny this honestly. "I had a few suspicions, but I realized after I got here that it wasn't enough. I couldn't accuse Lisha like that, not before I had absolute proof."

"Yet you did it anyway," Lisha said, her eyes slits as she glowered at Laurel.

"Laurel has yet to actually accuse you of anything. And it is beyond gracious of her to refrain, considering the way you've treated her," Hank growled. "I'm going to give you one last chance, Lisha. Once and for all, did you do this? And think hard before you answer. If you lie, I will find out. You might be MIT bound, but you know your computer skills haven't surpassed mine."

"I'm not MIT bound. Because of *her*!" Lisha pointed a

shaking finger at Laurel. "We don't have the money anymore. My entire future is gone in a flash because of her and her husband. And what happens to her? She gets a brand-new lodge with her best friends. The talk of the town is about how she rebuilt herself from the ashes of her former life. How strong Laurel is. How brave. It's a bunch of BS. I had to do something to take it down. She has to be taken down!"

"Go inside, Lisha," Hank said, his voice deadly calm.

Lisha seemed to realize her father meant business. But Laurel was pretty sure she didn't realize how bad her situation really was. She could be in deep legal trouble for what she'd done.

The three of them watched as Lisha stomped into the house. Laurel wasn't sure about the Fields, but the shock of what had happened kept her speechless.

The three remained in silence a few moments longer before Alice turned to Laurel.

"I have no idea what to say," Alice said in a thin voice as she held onto the window frame of Laurel's car, eyes downcast in shame.

"Nothing. This was your daughter, not you. Just like you said you can't blame me for Bennie, I can't blame either of you for this. My friends won't either," Laurel assured them. "Honestly, I don't know that any of us will be able to blame Lisha either. She's been through a lot."

"That's no excuse," Hank said, glancing from the house to Laurel.

"It's not. But it does make it easier to understand." Laurel remembered how Riley had said he would be ready to pounce as soon as they had a perpetrator, but it didn't feel right to go after Lisha or the Fields. They had nothing extra for legal fees, thanks to Laurel's husband. "If you can assure us that Lisha is done with all of this, I think we can call it even. So far, no criminal lines have been crossed. We would have had to seek retribution in civil court. And although I'll have to make sure all the girls are on board with this plan, I'm pretty sure we'll be ready to put it all behind us. We just want to focus on running our business."

Laurel knew just how busy the rest of her friends were. The last thing they'd have time for was going after a hurt teenager. Nor would any of them want to.

"We don't deserve that," Alice said, her grief evident in the strain of her voice.

"Just like none of you deserved what Bennie did," Laurel said, meeting Alice's and then Hank's eyes. "If Lisha will work with us and help us figure out how and who she targeted, we'll try to undo the negatives. Honestly, we are able to get reservations pretty easily; they just kept canceling afterwards. So without the anti-campaign, I think we'll be just fine. Great, even."

"Lisha will do that and more," Hank assured her. "She'll create a new post telling the truth and send it to all of the people she targeted with those lies."

That seemed more than fair.

"I can't speak for all of us yet, but I'm pretty sure that will be agreeable," Laurel said, smiling and trying to show that she felt no animosity toward this poor couple. They'd already been through so much; she hated that they now had to deal with this, too.

"Thank you," Alice whispered as she leaned into the car to give Laurel a hug. "You are a better person than I am."

Laurel shook her head. "You forgave me for worse. All I did was prove I can return a kindness."

"And we'll always remember that kindness," Hank said.

Laurel's heart swelled. Things were going to be okay. She still felt terrible for Lisha, but Laurel had a feeling that once

Lisha worked through some of her misplaced anger, she would be okay as well.

Who would have thought that at the end of this, Laurel could feel so tenderhearted toward the one who had wronged her? And although things weren't anywhere near fixed for Rosebud Lodge, they were on their way.

Laurel felt about twenty pounds lighter. The Lodge just might have a future after all.

CHAPTER TWELVE

"HEY," Wells said from the breakfast nook as Hazel walked into the kitchen.

She'd been miserably nauseated for the first couple of days after chemo, but now, a week later, she was feeling just a step above crummy. Just in time to be injected with the poison once again today. Ever since her diagnosis, she'd felt like the butt of some sick joke.

"Hey to you," Hazel replied, surprised that Wells was still here. Granted, she'd been surprised by a lot of his actions recently.

The man was busy, in the middle of recording his latest album. Wells had never put his career on hold when he and Hazel were together, and it was almost awkward that he was doing so now, as well as just puzzling.

When he'd shown up with Chase right after her diagnosis, she'd suspected they'd be gone as soon as day one of chemo was over, especially once Dylan showed up.

Hazel's body warmed. Dylan. The man who had hardly left her side since she'd finally let him back into her life. She'd warned him through her nausea that she was going to lose all of her hair . . . not to mention all the other unpleasant side effects. But nothing had dissuaded him.

She'd considered the cold cap, an option for trying to keep her hair while doing chemo, but when she heard how painful it was, she just couldn't do it on top of the misery of chemo. Even if her vanity begged for her to at least try, her practicality won out. Hazel was going to be bald. She was already losing handfuls of hair each time she brushed. And she was trying to be okay with it, but she didn't expect her ex-boyfriend to feel the same way.

Yet he seemed to. Dylan hardly left her side, even though Hazel still insisted they weren't together.

"That's fine," he'd told her in that husky voice of his. "Doesn't mean I'll stop caring."

If Hazel hadn't been about to puke her guts out, she would have been awed at the sentiment. Scratch that, right now she *was* feeling pretty dang awed.

Hazel poured a bowl of cereal, one of the only foods she'd been able to stomach for the past week, and got out a spoon.

"So is this, like, a thing now?" Hazel pointed her spoon to Wells and then waved it to encompass her kitchen.

"Me being here?" Wells asked, quickly catching onto her train of thought. They had been married for a few decades, after all.

Hazel nodded. They needed to have this conversation sometime. Might as well be now.

"Do you mind?" Wells got up from the breakfast table to join Hazel at the island.

She hadn't expected that. Not that Wells wasn't a considerate person, but he was typically decisive. She'd assumed he'd already made up his mind, and she would have to live with it or argue with him about it, just as they'd done throughout their marriage.

"How long?" Hazel needed to know his plan before she could answer his question.

"As long as you need me," Wells said, surprising her. That couldn't be right.

"You mean as long as Hutch will let you stay," Hazel corrected, referring to Wells' manager.

"Hutch is already chomping at the bit. And I told him yesterday what I'll continue to tell him. I'm here. I'm staying as long as you need me," Wells replied.

His hand hovered above Hazel's as if he was going to take it. Still trying to process, she drew hers back. What was happening? Where had this man been while they were married?

"Chemo is still a couple of months."

Wells nodded.

"And then there could be surgery, radiation—this could go on for a long time, Wells." Hazel tried to make her point clear.

"I know. But you are the mother of my children, the only woman I've ever loved."

Hazel shook her head. He wasn't doing this now, not while she was sick. And when she had Dylan . . . kind of. Holy Hannah, her life was a mess.

"Speaking of those children," Hazel said, trying hard not to let Wells' words get to her, "What about school? Chase is enrolled in Nashville."

"We switched him to online for the foreseeable future."

Chase couldn't be happy about that, surely. He'd had to leave his girlfriend behind. Wells must have gotten his signals crossed.

"What about Kenna?" Hazel asked between bites of cereal.

"They're doing the long-distance thing for now. Although, I think he's on the verge of breaking up with her, and moving here would be a good excuse for that. He mentioned that she's being clingy, especially after he told her he needs to be here for his mom."

"Chase said that?" Hazel choked, no longer able to keep her emotions in check. She dropped her spoon as warmth spread through her chest. It was one thing to disregard what her ex said, but this was Chase. Her baby boy.

Wells nodded.

"So you guys are *here* here?" Hazel asked, wondering if she really understood.

"Chauffeur, nursemaid, cleaning person, and chef." Wells pointed to himself.

"I have a cleaning lady," Hazel said, cocking her head in disbelief.

"Who, thanks to me, now comes three times a week instead of once," Wells grinned. "See? I'm taking care of the cleaning."

Hazel chuckled. That felt more right than the rest of the conversation. That would be the way Wells cleaned.

"And you don't cook," Hazel added.

"I can order a mean pizza. Now with all of these ordering services, I'm on top of my game."

Hazel shook her head, but she guessed she could give Wells that as well. And she had to admit that when Dylan wasn't around, Wells was an acceptable nurse. As long as Hazel made it to the toilet to vomit.

"And your album?" Hazel asked, eyeing him closely. The Wells she had known put his music above all else.

"On hold for the time being. We've allowed the producers to move on, and they've all promised to come back when the time is right."

"Seriously?" Hazel blinked. This kind of move had to be costing Wells' label hundreds of thousands of dollars, if not more.

"They owe it to me. Or at least that's what I told them. I've given them my all for the past twenty-four years. It's my turn to get what I need," Wells said, standing firm.

And what Wells needs is to be here? That was a can of worms Hazel planned to keep closed for the time being. There was nothing else to argue and only one thing left to say.

"Fine," she agreed reluctantly.

Had she just agreed to let her ex live with her? She rubbed her forehead with her hand. But before she had time to second-guess her decision, the doorbell rang.

"I'll get it," Wells offered, taking a step toward the front door.

But despite her physical condition, Hazel beat him to it. She wasn't sure who was on the other side of the door, and she wasn't sure she wanted them greeted by her newest housemate.

"Dylan," Hazel breathed as she opened the door, but then remembered she wasn't dating the man. He was just . . . what was he? A friend who held her hair, tucked her into bed, and saw her every need met? Yeah, that.

Hazel refused to think about how ridiculous that was.

"What are you doing here?" she asked. Didn't Dylan know she had to leave in just a couple of minutes?

"Today's the day, right?" he asked as he entered. His friendly smile morphed into a scowl when he saw Wells just inside the kitchen.

But he somehow managed to turn his frown back into a smile before looking down at Hazel. "Treatment number two? I'm here to help you get ready and drive you."

"Dylan," Hazel began, unsure of whether she was giving in or arguing with him.

She wanted nothing more than to have Dylan by her side through this struggle, but that wasn't fair to him. They weren't dating, because she couldn't bear to make him stay when he saw what this cancer was going to do to her. She'd seen the pictures. The frail bodies with no hair, no strength. Or if she lost this battle entirely . . . nope, she wasn't going there. But this wasn't Dylan's fight. She wouldn't tie him to her now and force him to stay with her for that. She couldn't.

"She's already got a driver, bro," Wells said as he came out of the kitchen and joined them in the foyer, which felt smaller with every person who entered.

"Hey Mom!" Sterling bounded down the steps and into the even more cramped foyer. "How are you feeling?"

Hazel was all too happy to ignore the men who were filling the room with tension and focus on her boy.

"Good, for now," she said honestly. Part of her wondered if it would be better to hide all the hard sides of cancer from her boys. But she realized that wasn't fair to any of them. Her boys needed to know that their mother struggled, just like she needed to know they cared for her. Letting them all the way in was the only way to do that.

Sterling nodded, understanding that this session would once again weaken her.

"I wanted to give this to you before you left." Sterling held out a dainty silver chain with a tiny wooden bouquet of roses on the end.

"It's gorgeous," Hazel admired, turning the beautiful gift in her hands.

"I made it in woodshop," Sterling said, standing a little taller.

"You did not!" Hazel eyes widened. Her darling boy had made this?

"Not the chain," he answered with a laugh.

"I assumed that much. But it's incredible. You have a gift, Ster," Hazel replied. She clasped it around her throat, turning to look in the foyer mirror.

Sterling beamed. "I just wanted you to have a piece of me when you went in today, you know?" he said.

Hazel's throat swelled. Wordlessly she brought her boy—

who was now a good head taller than she was—into her arms, hugging him too tightly. He grunted.

"You are the best," Hazel said.

"Be sure to tell Chase that," Sterling teased before ducking out of Hazel's arms and leaving the room. She wasn't surprised that this was too much affection for him. Teenaged boys weren't big into that and he'd already given her more than she expected.

"Have you eaten?" Dylan asked as he led Hazel into the kitchen after Sterling. Wells followed them.

"Shoot, my cereal." Hazel sighed. She was sure it was now a soggy mess.

"How about we go to that smoothie place you love? We can drive through on our way to the hospital," Wells offered.

"That's a great idea. I'll take her on *our* way," Dylan countered. Hazel could have sworn he puffed up his chest.

Nope. This was too much, and she was done. No matter how worn out she felt, Hazel needed to take the reins of this situation before it spiraled out of control.

"Wells, I'm grateful you're willing to take me, but I think it would be better if you stuck around here with the boys," she said firmly. Wasn't that why Wells was staying here anyway? To be there for their children?

Dylan smirked at Wells.

"But, Dylan, you need to know that Wells is—" she swallowed and forced her next words out, "—living here for the foreseeable future. I know it's . . . well, it's strange, is what it is. But he wants to be here for me and our boys, so we're doing this, for now."

This time Wells smirked.

Dylan's face went white. "You guys are getting back together."

Hazel shook her head vehemently as Wells nodded.

"No, we aren't," Hazel said to Wells. Maybe a little more

loudly than she needed to. Looking at Dylan, she added, "We're friends. We're all friends."

That was all Hazel could handle for now. She was thankful for both men. She wouldn't be managing any of this well without them, so if they could just stop arguing, that would be great.

"We'll see about that," both men said in unison, staring each other down.

What had Hazel gotten herself into?

CHAPTER THIRTEEN

WEARILY, Kenzie took a box from the trunk of her car and began the long walk down the driveway to the small bungalow Raquel was renting behind Kenzie's landlord's home. It was an ideal arrangement, because even though the space inside wasn't the largest, it was just big enough for Raquel and the dogs while being affordable on her tight budget.

Raquel's emotions had been all over the place when it came to this move. One moment she would tell Kenzie she knew it was for the best. Bryan moving home was practically a miracle for Kenzie's marriage, and Raquel had no desire to stay in the home with Kenzie and Bryan, interfering with their reconciliation. But then she'd have moments of melancholy where she wished things were different. She'd say she knew it was selfish, but why couldn't the sisters live together, just the two of them forever?

So Kenzie wasn't sure which Raquel she was going to encounter when she brought these last boxes of stuff over. Raquel's move was complete. At this very moment, a host of cleaners were back at Kenzie's, trying to get rid of all the dog hair before Bryan moved home. Kenzie knew she couldn't make things perfect for her husband, but she could make it so that at least he wouldn't start sneezing his brains out the moment he entered the home.

"Kenzie!" Raquel squealed as Kenzie tapped the box against the screen door to knock. Kenzie was relieved to see she was getting exuberant Raquel today. The one who was excited to move out on her own in Rosebud. Justin, Mark, and Nick stood just behind their mom, barking their greetings to their human aunt.

Raquel opened the door, taking the box just in time, because the doggies weren't about to let Kenzie enter their new home without loving on her first.

Kenzie knelt to give each dog a hug and realized that even though Raquel's moving out was for the best, she really was going to miss these adorable boybanders. If Kenzie was being honest, the canine versions might even be cuter than their human inspirations.

"I have two more in the car, and that should be the last of it," Kenzie said as she attempted to free herself from the enthusiastic dogs and navigate her way to the couch. The three dogs wound around her feet, letting her know they weren't going to leave her side.

"It's just so sad, isn't it?" Raquel asked as she set down the box on the kitchen counter and sighed. Raquel's new place basically consisted of two square rooms. The first was the one they stood in, a combination living room and kitchen. The kitchen island doubled as a dining table. The second square was the enormous bedroom she'd share with her boys, plus a decent-sized bathroom just off it. The cottage was tiny, but it had everything Raquel could need. And it was cheap. Considering Raquel had yet to find a job, cheap was exactly what she needed.

"What's so sad?" Kenzie realized that melancholy Raquel

had returned. *Shoot.* She really shouldn't have asked Raquel to dwell on her sadness and instead started pointing out the good.

"Us. Not living together anymore," Raquel replied with a frown.

Okay, it was time to turn this conversation around. Kenzie could have pointed out that they'd lived together for barely over a month. Or the fact that if Raquel had stayed any longer, one of them might have killed the other. Kenzie loved her sister, but there was a reason siblings hardly ever lived together after age eighteen. Those relationships were typically better at a distance.

"It is. But this is great for you." Kenzie tried to lift her sister's spirits.

"Yeah." Raquel looked around her cute place. "It is kind of perfect. And the boys already love the king-size bed."

"We knew they would," Kenzie said. She'd gone house hunting with Raquel when it was evident her sister wasn't going to do anything about moving out until Kenzie made her. The housing market, especially for rentals, wasn't exactly robust in Rosebud, but Raquel hadn't wanted to move out of town. She said now that she was getting older, she needed to be closer to those she loved . . . just not too close to their parents. Thankfully, they'd found this ideal spot, and as long as Raquel found a new job soon, she would be set.

"Oh, and Kenz! I can't believe I nearly forgot to tell you. I've been saving the best news until I saw you in person." Raquel grabbed her sister's hands and pulled her down on the couch with her. "I got a job!"

Kenzie breathed a sigh of relief. That was the last missing piece. A part of her had worried that Raquel would be back in her spare room before the month was out if she hadn't found one, so this was incredible news.

"I went to the Lodge like you suggested," Raquel explained with a wide smile.

Kenzie's excitement abated a bit. When they'd first talked about job searching, Kenzie had suggested that Raquel go to Callie. She knew there had been a couple of housekeeping and grounds positions that didn't require previous experience. But those had been filled before Raquel got around to it. Had Callie found something for Raquel even though they didn't actually need her? *Dang it.* Kenzie hadn't meant to put her friend in this position. She'd have to call and apologize later; she hadn't even given Callie a heads-up because Raquel had said those jobs were beneath her when Kenzie had first mentioned them.

"I'm glad Callie found something for you," Kenzie said with a grin, mustering as much enthusiasm as she could. So Raquel hadn't done things exactly the way Kenzie had suggested. That was no reason for Kenzie not to be thrilled for her sister. She had found a job, and that was what mattered.

"Oh, not Callie. I could never clean someone else's room." Raquel shuddered. "I went to Saffron. We got to talking, and I told her that you suggested I would be perfect for any job at the Lodge thanks to my vast work experience."

Kenzie felt a lump growing in her throat. Had she said that? She seriously doubted it, considering that she didn't really think Raquel would be perfect for *any* job. Maybe Kenzie had said something vaguely along those lines, and Raquel had taken a bit of license with her words. The reason Raquel had so much 'work experience' was because she was often fired within her first few months at a job. If she lasted longer than that, she typically quit. And now that flighty sister was going to be working in their kitchen? It was one thing to have Raquel cleaning rooms with a supervisor like Callie. But working in the kitchen, under Saffron?

"You don't cook," Kenzie spouted the obvious, trying not to appear as ruffled as she felt.

"I don't clean either, and yet you wanted me to take that housekeeping job."

Raquel wasn't wrong. But that didn't make this situation any better. Saffron had hired Raquel as a favor to Kenzie, thinking that she had requested it. What was she going to do?

"Raquel, this isn't like your other jobs. This Lodge is everything to me and my friends. Things are finally going well for us, and I need you to . . . " Kenzie paused. She wanted to say that she wanted Raquel to work harder than she ever had, but she knew her sister would take offense at the implication that she didn't typically work hard. "Bring your A game," she finished. Hopefully, that was a strong enough admonition.

"Of course. I always do," Raquel said, scrunching up her dark brows.

Nope. That wouldn't work. Raquel could not treat this the way she treated other jobs.

"I understand that. But, Raquel, I need more than you normally bring. I need you to go into this as if you've invested all of your savings with your very best friends. As if the people you love most in the world could lose their livelihood if you don't kill it every day at work," Kenzie replied. "Because that's what could really happen."

"You do understand that I'll probably just be peeling potatoes and stuff, right?" Raquel asked, cocking her head.

"And I wouldn't trust anyone else to peel those potatoes better," Kenzie replied, realizing that maybe she was overreacting a bit. Raquel had found a job, just like she'd promised. So what if the job wasn't exactly what Kenzie had envisioned?

Kenzie would talk to Saffron and tell her to treat Raquel like any other employee, not to keep her on just because she was Kenzie's sister. And then she would hope that Raquel really would do what she was promising.

It would all work out.

"I get it, Sis. I do. This is a big deal for all of you. I'm just happy that I get to have a small part in it. And I promise to do my part well," Raquel said.

"Thank you." Kenzie smiled at her sister. For all of her flakiness, Raquel was loyal to a fault to the people she truly cared about. Kenzie had hopes for that loyalty, and that this would be just the thing to bring some stability into her sister's life.

"Now do you mind getting those last two boxes? I met this guy at the bank this morning, and he's taking me out tonight," Raquel said as she stood.

"Fun. What's his name?" Rosebud was a small town. There was a good chance Kenzie had at least heard of Raquel's date.

"Bobby. No, Buddy. No, definitely Bobby." Raquel frowned and then shrugged. "I'll just wait to say it until he mentions it again or someone else does."

And there was the other side of her sister she knew and loved. Kenzie laughed. Her sister was making big strides. Just maybe not in every part of her life.

CHAPTER FOURTEEN

THE CLUMPS of hair on the bathroom counter seemed to mock Hazel. Thousands of blonde strands gone. She'd been brushing so gently, trying to keep this exact thing from happening even though she knew the inevitable end.

But once the hair had started filling her brush, it didn't seem to stop. Every few strokes Hazel had to stop and clear out the hair. Then she'd go back to brushing, slowly and painstakingly, but there were so many tangles. When one was gone another seemed to appear, until there was so much hair on the counter Hazel couldn't bring herself to look in the mirror.

Her hair had begun thinning after her very first session of chemo, but then it had seemed to stall. She was still losing hair but was keeping enough that she hoped she was one of the lucky cases, one of the few who could go through chemo and keep their hair.

Hazel had never thought of her hair as integral to who she was until it had begun to fall out. Her hair had always been rather long, falling over her shoulders. She realized it had become a part of her identity, and even though it felt silly caring about her hair when she was fighting for her life, she did care. A lot.

Hazel finally looked up, her eyes meeting her reflection in the mirror. She locked her gaze on her own blue eyes. They'd been brighter in years past. Clearer, maybe even more blue. But the graying blue was still pretty. A part of her she could still take pride in.

In contrast, her skin seemed to have aged years in the past couple of chemo sessions. Her wrinkles appeared more pronounced, and she wasn't sure if it was just her imagination, but her cheeks seemed to be sagging.

She knew it wasn't helping that she was losing weight, but the nausea of chemo was killing her. She could hardly eat for days after each session and just as she got her appetite back, it would be time for another round.

She was exhausted. And she looked it.

Finally her gaze lifted to her hairline. It was farther back than it had been even a week before. And then as she allowed herself to take in her entire head, the loss of her hair was painfully obvious. She pulled a few strands to one side, leaning closer to the mirror. A bald patch, at least the size of a quarter.

Her stomach clenched.

This was it. It was really going to all fall out.

The idea of waiting for that torturous process to take place was too much. But what alternative did she have?

She could shave her head right now.

Hazel scoffed at her reflection. No. Some hair was better than no hair.

But then she imagined another round of doing this exact thing. Brushing her hair carefully and slowly only to have what felt like half of the remaining strands fall out. Could she do that? Did she want to do that?

Did she want to allow this poison in her veins, the very

thing that was helping her fight for her life but was killing other parts of her, to kill off every last hair follicle? To watch helplessly as yet another thing was taken from her?

Or did she want to give it up on her own terms?

She knew many shaved their head before this point. She'd already held on longer than most. Maybe it was because she was more vain. She hated to admit to her vanity, but she'd always been called a beauty. Over time she guessed she'd started to believe it. It had become a part of her very identity, the fabric that made Hazel, Hazel. So could she be herself without her hair? With the cornerstone of her beauty ripped away?

Honestly, the idea of losing her beauty wasn't as hard as the idea of the pity she'd receive from others when they saw she'd lost her hair. She didn't want pity. She didn't need pity. What she needed was to feel like Hazel again.

And then she knew. Hazel kicked down doors; she didn't wait for trouble to come to her. She had always been the author of her own story, so maybe that was why this was so difficult. Cancer had taken the pen out of her hand for the last months. But Hazel was ready to take it back.

She could still be beautiful without hair. And over the past few months, her beauty had mattered to her less and less. Cancer had a way of putting things into perspective.

And with this new perspective, she was going to shave her head.

Hazel walked out of her bathroom before she lost her nerve. Being a mom of boys, she had a couple of hair clippers around her home.

She went to the hall closet and opened the door, staring down the black case that would help her to take charge of her life once again. She wouldn't have chosen to lose her hair. But now that the choice had been made for her, she was going to choose to lose it today. In her own time, in her own home, in her own way.

"Mom?" Chase asked as he encountered his mom in the middle of the hall, staring into a random closet.

She knew she must look half crazed, but Chase had been her son for long enough to know his mother had these moments. Especially since she'd been diagnosed.

She glanced at him and sure enough, he looked more curious than concerned.

"Can you grab those for me?" Hazel requested, pointing to the black case that was just beyond her reach. It had been a blessed day when her boys both passed her five-foot-four frame. Now they could reach all of the things she couldn't. Human stools at their best.

Chase looked from the case that held the hair clippers to his mom's head.

"Are you sure?" he asked softly.

It showed how much he'd grown in the last few months. When they'd moved home to Rosebud, Chase would have been too self-absorbed, like most teenagers, to notice the turmoil Hazel was experiencing. But since he'd gone to Nashville and then returned with Wells to Rosebud after Hazel's diagnosis, Chase had been more aware. Almost too grown-up.

Hazel was of two minds about the changes in her oldest. As much as she appreciated them, she didn't like that Chase had made them because of her cancer. She wanted him to grow up in his own time.

Then again, who was Hazel to determine Chase's own time? Navigating parenting after a cancer diagnosis had been frustrating, to say the least. Not because of her boys—they'd been as close to being angels as healthy, active boys could—but because Hazel felt now more than ever that she wasn't enough for them.

But she'd come to realize that all she could do was her best. So she was trying. And failing. But then trying again. She figured for now it was all she could do.

Hazel nodded.

Chase reached up and easily brought down the case holding the hair clippers. He eyed the piece of plastic in his hands carefully.

"Do you want me to do it for you?" he asked, still looking at the case.

Hazel felt a lump form in her throat. This might be the kindest thing anyone had ever offered her. But she couldn't ask that of Chase. Doing it for herself would be hard enough.

"I'd like to do it," Chase added. He raised his eyes, moving his careful gaze to her.

Hazel swallowed.

"I can't ask you to do that," she said, her eyes stinging. She would not cry.

"You're not asking," Chase said, gently pushing his mom in the direction of her bathroom and following behind.

"Chase, you don't have to do this," Hazel reiterated, trying to grab the case out of Chase's hands.

"I want to," he insisted, easily evading her reach.

Hazel studied her older son, the boy who'd made her a mom, the child she was supposed to be protecting. Would this be too much for him?

But as she examined him she realized something she'd missed up until that moment. The boy had broader shoulders and had grown a head taller than his mom. He'd had so many physical changes over the years, but as Hazel looked into his eyes she saw that her little boy had become a man. A man who wanted to be a support for his mother.

"Thank you," Hazel answered huskily as she tried to swallow back her overwhelming emotion.

She leaned against the bathroom counter, ignoring the pile of hair behind her, as Chase plugged in the clippers. He carefully detached the safety clip. There was no need to worry about lengths. Hazel needed to shave everything to the nub. It would all be gone soon anyway.

"I used to resent that all of my friends thought you were such a hot mom," Chase began as he cleaned the hair that lingered in the clippers from the last person who'd used it. Probably himself.

Hazel chuckled. "Is it a relief to know I won't be the hot mom anymore?" she joked.

Chase shook his head. "That was never it. Mom, you'll be beautiful no matter what you do. Without hair, eyebrows, eyelashes. Losing twenty pounds. Drowning in your clothes, you're beautiful."

"You don't have to say that," Hazel said softly, even as she savored the words. For anyone to think she could still be beautiful after all of this was the buoy she needed as she treaded water in this sea of uncertainty.

"You will be. But that's not my point. My point is that I hated that my friends all thought you were the hot mom because you've always been so much more than your looks. I wanted them to see you. Mom. The woman who stayed up late with me for three weeks straight just to study for a math test that I still bombed. Do you remember what you said after I came home with a D?"

Hazel shook her head. She vaguely remembered being so tired she could barely function, but she had forgotten that Chase had failed that test. She'd just been so proud of how hard he'd worked.

"You said that D was worth more than a dozen A's that I didn't work for."

Hazel smiled. That sounded like something she would say. She really had been impressed with his work ethic.

"That's who you've always been, Mom. The hard-working woman who does things behind the scenes. You never do stuff for praise, and you're happy letting everyone else stand in the limelight, especially Dad. You are brave, and the way you're doing this proves it once again." He smirked suddenly. "And you don't take crap from anyone."

"Don't say *crap*," Hazel said, losing her battle against her tears. Hearing what Chase thought of her was more than she could have ever wished for. This from the boy who had declared that he hated her when she had initially refused to let him live with his dad?

"You don't. Not even from me. And we all know I like to dish it."

Hazel chuckled through her tears.

"So as much as I know you're going to hate this, you can do it. But I won't let you do it alone," Chase said defiantly, as if his words could keep the cancer at bay.

Hazel let out a sob, her emotions overwhelming her.

"Happy tears," she assured Chase when his face filled with alarm.

He grinned.

"Good. You ready?" He held up the clippers, his face growing serious.

Hazel set her jaw and nodded, and Chase turned them on. The buzzing sound filled the entire bathroom.

Chase paused, the clippers just at the edge of Hazel's hairline. She nodded again and Chase began, the first swipe making a clean cut through Hazel's remaining hair. There was now officially no need to worry about a single bald patch.

Hazel felt tears streaming silently down her cheeks, a mixture of sadness and happiness as Chase continued to shave.

And then it was over. She glanced down to see strands that had fallen to the ground.

"Who knew your head was so pale," Chase said.

Hazel looked up in surprise, meeting Chase's teasing eyes in the mirror.

"You'll need to find some really good sunscreen," he continued.

Hazel let out a shaky laugh. Count on Chase to know when she needed a good laugh.

"What's going on in . . . " Sterling peeked his head into the bathroom and froze when he saw what Chase was doing.

"It's time?" he asked after a few moments of silence as he absorbed the scene.

Chase nodded.

Sterling stepped into the bathroom, leaning his back against the wall behind him.

Hazel felt even lighter. The support Sterling was lending was nearly as helpful as Chase shaving her head for her.

"Chase was telling me I need to get some good sunscreen for my pale head," Hazel said. She didn't look at them as she spoke. It hurt her too much to see the pain in both of her boys' eyes.

They'd been knocked down by her diagnosis and just when they'd begun to bounce back, the chemo sickness had hit. Now that they'd gotten used to that, there was a new blow. Hazel's loss of her hair was yet another glaring, physical reminder that she wasn't well. It wasn't fair.

Sterling chuckled. "Maybe Chase can lend you the stuff he uses for his face. I've never seen anyone care so much about their skincare regimen," Sterling teased his big brother.

"Don't come crying to me in twenty years when you look forty and I look twenty-five," Chase said with a shrug as he shaved off the very last line of Hazel's hair.

Hazel stared at her reflection. Not a single strand remained, and an alien mound of head greeted her. Chase was right that it was pale. Extremely so.

But she guessed she didn't look bad. Tentatively she rubbed her smooth head. Different, but different wasn't bad. It was just . . . different. She knew she would mourn her hair but right now she felt okay. She was going to be okay. Shaving her head had been the best thing she could have done in this situation. She did feel empowered because she'd made her own decision, wresting control back from her illness.

Sterling drew in a sharp breath, pulling her gaze from her own reflection to Sterling's behind her.

"What . . . " Hazel began to ask as her eyes shifted to Chase's reflection. Her voice trailed off in shock.

He was missing a stripe of hair, right down the middle of his head.

"Chase," Hazel whispered as she reached toward his head, stopping short of touching him. His hair was beautiful. The kind of blonde that women spent hundreds a month trying to replicate, with a perfect wave that made all of the girls in his class swoon.

"I just wanted to see if it was as pale as yours," Chase said, pointing at his scalp. "I think I might have you beat."

Hazel shook her head wordlessly, battling pride, concern, and an overabundance of love.

"Did you really think I was going to let you do this by yourself?" Chase asked as Sterling grabbed the clippers and in one fell swoop shaved his own stripe through the middle of his black, luscious locks.

"Sterling!" Hazel gasped.

"I can't let him do this alone and become the favorite son," Sterling retorted with a grin. He turned from side to side. "I actually kind of like this look."

"You do realize I already am the favorite son," Chase said.

He snatched the clippers back and continued shaving his head. Soon he was as bald as Hazel.

"You wish," Sterling muttered, folding his arms and waiting for his turn.

Hazel laughed. She couldn't believe her boys were doing this for her. She knew she'd cry because of them tonight. This gesture could not be topped. But she knew they'd be uncomfortable if she started crying now so with an effort she composed herself, saving her tears until she was on her own.

She watched, mesmerized, as Chase finished his hair and passed the clippers to Sterling.

"Do you think we can convince Dad to shave his head too?" Sterling asked when half of his hair was gone. He looked ridiculous—black curls covering one side of his head, white scalp on the other. And Hazel loved him so much for it.

"Dad?" Chase asked, eyes wide. "Yeah, right."

"He'd do it for mom," Sterling argued as he continued.

"That's true," Chase agreed.

It wasn't often her boys agreed, so Hazel tried not to appear alarmed, especially considering the subject matter. What did they mean by that?

But now wasn't the time to reflect on their meaning. Now was the time to love on her sweet boys, the boys she didn't deserve but thanked God for every day.

Sterling turned off the clippers a few minutes later and set them down. He stood on one side of Hazel. Chase had moved to the other to allow Sterling to get closer to the mirror while he shaved.

Hazel took in their three bare scalps.

"You two," she said, looking from one precious son to the other.

"You're wondering how we look so ridiculously handsome, even without hair," Chase said with a grin.

Hazel laughed.

"Something like that," she said as she put an arm around each of her sons and pulled them close.

"I really do look pretty danged amazing," Sterling said, tilting his neck this way and that to take in his reflection.

Hazel knew the overconfidence was all a show. Their eyes told the truth. Her boys were nervous, but they didn't regret what they had done. For her.

"There has never been a luckier mom," she said, squeezing her boys.

"She isn't wrong," Chase said as Sterling said, "I agree."

Hazel laughed. Maybe she wasn't doing everything right as a mom, but in moments like this she realized none of that mattered. What mattered was this. These moments. And she would savor this particular one forever.

CHAPTER FIFTEEN

"HAVE a great stay at the Rosebud Lodge," Callie said with a grin as she pressed a keycard into the hand of their latest guest.

They only had two empty rooms that evening. And by the next weekend, each and every guest suite should be full. Callie couldn't believe what a difference a few weeks had made.

After Laurel had uncovered who was behind the smear campaign and the Lodge's lost reservations, the rest of the girls had been upset for about two minutes before they realized the same thing Laurel had. The campaign had simply been the actions of a young, hurting girl.

Since then, Lisha had spent countless hours trying to undo the harm of her negative advertising, and in return, Laurel had started a fund for Lisha's college expenses. Laurel had promised the girl she'd help her get to MIT if she would use all of her extensive brain power for good. Lisha had cried at that point, telling Laurel she didn't deserve the second chance, but Laurel had insisted she had.

Lisha's parents had been less forgiving. It sounded like Lisha was grounded until the moment she left for college.

But between Lisha's efforts and the marketing prowess of

Callie, Laurel, and Kenzie, things at the Lodge were finally turning around. And for that, Callie could not feel more grateful, even if it had taken a while to get there.

"Special delivery," Kenzie called as she brought a vase of flowers to the front desk that Callie was manning that afternoon. Even though reservations were increasing, the girls were still doing as much of the work as they could on their own. They would eventually hire more employees, but for now it still made fiscal sense for them to do all they could.

Callie gazed at the flowers. She didn't have to read the card to know who had sent them. Things with Leo were going smoothly. Actually, more than smoothly. He made time for her every day, even if it was just a few texts, and he loved to spoil her with bouquets of flowers at least once a week. How had she gotten so lucky?

As soon as Kenzie set down the vase, Callie leaned into the blue and white blooms, taking in their fragrance. Leo tried hard to find flowers that were in season and wonderfully scented. Callie hadn't realized it before she became a regular recipient of bouquets, but fragrance meant much more to her than appearance.

"I think Bryan needs to take a few lessons from Leo," Kenzie said as she eyed the beautiful bouquet and took a turn sniffing the flowers when Callie had gotten her fill.

"Pretty sure Bryan is doing a few things right, though," Callie teased.

It had been a long time since Callie had seen Kenzie smile as much as she had in the past few weeks since her husband had moved home. Sure, they still had their ups and downs, but they both claimed their counselor was their best secret weapon to having a good marriage, and Kenzie was deliriously happy. Bryan seemed to be as well.

"He is," Kenzie acknowledged, her face glowing like a

newlywed. There was something delightful about rediscovering love.

"How's Raquel doing?" Callie asked in a whisper, unsure whether Kenzie's sister was working that afternoon.

"According to Saff, she's doing really well. I made Saffron promise not to sugarcoat anything, but it sounds like peeling potatoes was my sister's unknown calling. Other than asking Raquel to flirt less with the other kitchen staff, Saffron says working with Raquel has been a dream," Kenzie said with a wide grin. It was easy to see she was proud of her sister.

"Wait, did Raquel flirt with Alex?" Callie asked, raising her eyebrows.

She knew things were weird between Saffron and her handsome sous chef. It was plain to see they were attracted to each other. Saffron even went over to Alex's house one night a week —supposedly only to spend time with Alex's mom. But when it came to dating, they were seeing everyone but each other.

"I think so," Kenzie said, cringing. "Of course, Saffron would never outright say it, but that was the vibe I got."

Callie frowned. "Do you think those two will ever realize they're perfect for one another?"

"We can only hope," Kenzie sighed. She glanced up as another set of guests came through the front doors. "See you at Hazel's tonight?"

"Wouldn't miss it," Callie said, putting on a welcoming smile for the guests as Kenzie made herself scarce.

CHAPTER SIXTEEN

LAUREL STOOD in front of Lisha's home with a gigantic check in her hands. She knew the gesture was over the top. There was no need for the fake check to accompany the actual dollar figure in the bank account—the bank account that now held enough for Lisha's entire first year at MIT. A video that Laurel's daughter Mari had posted had gone viral: two million views in just a few days.

The video had been silly. Mari had recorded Laurel advocating for Lisha. Laurel had explained what had happened and the role she felt she'd played in the demise of Lisha's dreams. She had spoken passionately from her heart, with no idea that her daughter was taking a video.

And then Mari had posted it to her account without Laurel's knowledge, linking the Venmo where Laurel was collecting donations for Lisha's tuition.

During a visit to the post office two mornings later the postmaster had shown Laurel the video and Laurel had been mortified. She had been about to ask Mari to take down the video when she'd checked the amount in the Venmo account. It had doubled since Laurel had last checked, just a day before.

She checked again a few hours later, and the funds had doubled again. Money had poured in from around the world, with cute messages of encouragement attached. Laurel had collected those messages for Lisha and made a little notebook of them. Anytime Lisha felt overwhelmed or ready to give up while she was away at college, she could look at the words and remember that her college dreams were bigger than just herself.

"No!" Alice gasped as she raced out of her doorway, dishtowel in hand.

Laurel realized she'd been lollygagging on the front lawn so long that Alice had spied her through the windows. She didn't want Lisha to do the same. She wanted to see her face when the girl found out she would still get to attend the college of her dreams.

Laurel nodded her head, tears filling her eyes. She hadn't been sure she should be the one to give Lisha this check. Helping Lisha had been about so much more than Laurel. But there was really no one else to do it. Most of the donations had come from people Lisha would never know. That was what was even more magnificent about this all.

"Lisha is going to freak out. *I* am freaking out," Alice said as she wrung the towel. "I just can't believe it. How?"

Laurel chuckled. "That silly video I told you I was going to kick Mari's cute little behind for posting," she explained.

Alice's eyes went wide. "The power of social media," she muttered.

"I'd say," Laurel agreed. "But I'd better come in before Lisha spies this the same way you did."

Alice nodded and stepped aside to let Laurel in, disbelief still spelled all over her features. She suddenly pulled Laurel to a stop. "I don't know that Lisha deserves this. When you started this fund I thought it was a kind gesture. But I never expected it to come through. For Lisha to have all she needs for

MIT. Part of me wonders if she needs to be punished more for what she's done," Alice said, dropping her voice. It was obvious she didn't want her innermost thoughts overheard by her family.

"She's been punished so much already, Alice. None of this would have happened if it weren't for Bennie. Did Lisha react like she should have? No. But I can't say I blame her. She felt like she had nothing to lose."

"And she hurt you and your friends beyond repair."

"Not beyond repair at all. We're recovering just fine. In fact, this viral video has also gotten us quite a few new reservations at the Lodge, which wouldn't have happened unless Lisha had sabotaged our first marketing attempts. So Lisha is actually responsible for the Lodge doing better than it might have if this whole thing hadn't happened," Laurel countered, moving toward the doorway again.

Alice joined her and glanced to her side, taking in Laurel and the check.

"So you're trying to tell me that unless Lisha had sabotaged your Lodge, you wouldn't have made this video, and because of this video you all are doing better than ever? So somehow Lisha is the reason you're doing better than ever?" Alice said skeptically.

"Exactly. Now don't you think she deserves this?" Laurel asked with a wink.

Alice laughed and shook her head as they paused on her front porch. "I guess so. This started when Lisha was punished by actions beyond her control. I guess for her to be rewarded by that same type of thing is just desserts."

"I couldn't agree more." Laurel hugged her friend with her free arm and then followed Alice into her living room.

"What's that?" asked Beck, one of Alice's younger kids, as he pointed to the check in Laurel's hands. Laurel was just grateful he was too young to read or she was sure he'd be broadcasting the message for everyone in the house.

"Can you get Lisha, please?" Alice asked, sidestepping the question.

Beck looked from the check to his mom, probably realizing he wouldn't get his answer unless he did as she asked. Smart kid.

Beck ran toward the bedrooms, screaming, "Lisha!"

Alice glanced over at Laurel and rolled her eyes.

"You're going to miss these days," Laurel promised. She knew she did.

"You sure about that?" Alice asked and both women laughed.

"Lisha!" Beck screamed once again.

"What?" Lisha responded after the second call.

"A lady is here to see you!" Beck's voice seemed to get louder by the word. Laurel wondered if the neighbors could hear the exchange.

"Coming!" Lisha called back.

Alice just shook her head as if this was nothing new.

Suddenly self-conscious, Laurel stuck the giant check behind her back. She wasn't sure why. It wasn't like her body could hide the enormous piece of cardboard, but she did it just as Lisha rounded the corner and entered the living room.

"Hey, Laurel," Lisha greeted with a huge smile. Long gone were the glares. Smiles were all Laurel ever got now from this sweet girl.

Lisha seemed to be hurting less after coming clean about her sabotage against the Lodge, but Laurel knew that behind all of her smiles she still feared for her future. Even as she hoped in Laurel's attempts to regain her college money, Lisha knew it was a long shot. And she had come to accept that. Laurel could see it by the way her eyes were just a bit dimmer each time she saw her. It was almost like each interaction reminded her how unlikely going to MIT was for her, as the time for starting college drew closer and closer but the funds hadn't come.

"I've got an idea for a new marketing concept. I think Callie is going to love it," Lisha said. She stopped as she spotted the gigantic piece of cardboard Laurel was trying to hide. Her eyes filled with interest.

Lisha seemed just as curious as her brother, who now pushed behind Laurel to get a better view of the check.

"You've been working so hard. Thank you," Laurel said genuinely. She'd never seen a person more remorseful for their actions. Especially one who'd been so belligerent just a couple weeks before.

"Not hard enough. I'll never be able to make it up to you," Lisha said, her curiosity changing to regret as her eyes dropped to the ground.

"Ah, well, I'm not so sure about that," Laurel said with a grin.

Lisha looked up as Alice sat on the nearest couch, her grin nearly as wide as Laurel's.

"You saw that video, right?" Laurel started, knowing that every teenager in town had to have seen it. It had gone viral on a variety of social media platforms.

Lisha laughed. "The one of you lamenting about how unfair life is for me? Yeah. I bet like a million of those views are kids from my school. They think it's awesome."

Laurel joined in her laughter, still feeling embarrassed about it all, especially now that she knew it was the talk of the high school. She had pretty much made a fool of herself. She hadn't realized Mari was filming and had been mortified when she realized she had. So much so that Laurel had yet to watch the video. She only had her memories of living the moment, and they were more than enough.

"Awesome . . . or ridiculous," Laurel said when her laughter abated. "Anyway, it got like two million views."

"Three million now," Lisha said as she pulled up the video.

"What?" Laurel leaned in to see Lisha's phone. Sure enough, the views had gone up again. Laurel smiled, realizing there was probably more in Lisha's fund than even this check represented.

"You're a star, Laurel. I wouldn't be surprised if GMA came a-calling," Lisha teased.

Alice chuckled and Laurel smiled. No way would she be doing any kind of interviews. Unless it would help Lisha . . . or the Lodge. Dang it. She saw interviews in her future. She tried not to scowl but instead focused on the great part of this—she would get to gift this check to Lisha.

"Did you know that video was linked to your Venmo?" Laurel asked.

"*Your* Venmo," Lisha corrected.

"The account I set up for you," Laurel said.

"About that. I'm not sure. I've been thinking about it and it doesn't feel right to profit from what I did."

"I'm just restoring what you lost because of me," Laurel countered.

"Because of your *husband*. Not you. Huge difference," Lisha replied, showing what a long way she'd come since the day she'd called Laurel trash for being associated with Bennie.

Lisha was right, but Laurel's guilt didn't seem to agree. She had to make Lisha and her family understand.

"You know how you feel about what you did?" Laurel asked.

"Horrible? Yeah," Lisha acknowledged.

"That's the same way I feel about what Bennie did," Laurel admitted.

"You shouldn't," Lisha and Alice said in unison.

"That doesn't change how I feel."

"So giving me the viral money will make you feel better?" Lisha asked, raising an eyebrow.

"Incredibly," Laurel replied.

Lisha pursed her lips. "Is that a gigantic check behind you?" she asked. Clearly she wasn't just book smart. MIT would be lucky to have her.

Laurel nodded, feeling like she was caught red-handed even though she was just doing something nice.

The corners of Lisha's lips lifted. "I've always wanted to get a gigantic check."

"Right?" Laurel laughed, feeling so much better.

"And it's not like the viral video made that much, right? People never put their money where their views are," Lisha said. She stopped talking as Laurel pulled out the check and showed Lisha the number that said people very much did put their money where their views were.

Lisha's mouth dropped open.

"No," she gasped, tears filling her eyes.

"Yes," Laurel said softly.

"It's too much," Lisha said through her tears. She dropped her face into her hands.

"It's exactly what you need for your first year at MIT, room and board included. I looked it up," Laurel said, feeling tears well in her own eyes. "And who knows? There's probably more now since the video is still getting views."

Lisha shook her head and wiped her eyes, stepping back from the check. "No. That money should go to you. The Lodge. I can't take it."

"Lisha, the Lodge is doing better than we could have imagined—in part due to this video. Because of what you did, the Lodge is thriving."

"No, the Lodge is thriving despite what I did. It's because of what *you* did." Lisha looked at Laurel and then glanced back at the check. Laurel knew it had to be killing her to deny herself this chance.

"I wouldn't have made the video if it weren't for you," Laurel said. "Lisha, please. I can't and won't take this money. People wanted *you* to have it."

Laurel handed Lisha the book of messages that had come with the money.

Lisha took the book but held it away from herself like she wasn't sure what to do with it.

"Open it," Laurel encouraged.

Lisha slowly opened the book and began reading aloud. "Only geniuses go to MIT. Glad to support a genius." Lisha laughed through her tears. "I couldn't go to college because I had to care for my sick mom. Go to college for me, girl."

Lisha paused and looked at Laurel, her face filled with wonder.

"There are nearly a hundred just like that," Laurel said.

Lisha shook her head. "I don't deserve it."

"Your remorse is inspiring, Lisha. You could have chosen to stay mad at me. Now we're friends."

"You're a heck more than a friend if you hand me money like this," Lisha stated. Laurel smiled at the first indication that the girl's determination to refuse the money was wavering.

"Besides, my mom and dad were the ones who made me apologize," Lisha added.

"But no one could make you mean it," Laurel replied.

Lisha sat very still, knowing Laurel was right. Finally she took a deep breath.

"If I take this," Lisha began slowly. Laurel grinned. "If," Lisha added emphatically when she saw Laurel's grin. "This is it. No more money. I've earned some scholarships, and I was planning on entering the work-study program. I also qualify for financial aid and can get a loan if needed, so after this year I'll do it on my own. The rest of the money goes to the others."

Lisha didn't need to tell Laurel who the others were. So many had been burned by Bennie.

"Okay. But you get to help me decide who the money goes to," Laurel compromised.

Lisha nodded.

"Then you'll take it?" Laurel asked, scooting the check toward Lisha.

Lisha nodded, tears streaming down her cheeks.

"I'm going to MIT," she said softly and then pushed the check out of the way to hug Laurel. "I'm going to MIT," she screamed. Laurel winced, wondering if she might be a little hard of hearing in that ear for a few days, but it was worth it.

Lisha was going to MIT.

CHAPTER SEVENTEEN

"FOR SHE'S A JOLLY GOOD FELLOW," Saffron belted out. Hazel quickly hushed her.

"That is truly a terrible song to sing to a woman. And your voice isn't much better," Hazel teased, letting the girls know she was in perfect form that evening.

At first it had been a bit startling to see Hazel free of hair. Callie hadn't even seen her with a short haircut before, since she'd always kept it long. But like everything else, Hazel wore the look with ease and still was the most gorgeous woman in the room.

Callie had even caught a glimpse of Sterling's and Chase's bald heads. They looked adorable and according to Hazel were more popular than ever with the ladies after they'd heard the reason the boys had shaved their heads.

The girls had come over to celebrate Hazel's impromptu haircut as well as the fact that she'd officially reached the halfway point of her chemo treatments. At least her pre-surgery treatments. They weren't sure what steps came after surgery; it would depend on how much of the cancer the surgeons were able to eradicate. But the girls had decided that they were going to celebrate every milestone and win with Hazel. She'd already been through so much. She deserved this and so much more.

"My voice is just fine, thank you," Saffron said in mock indignation as she filled champagne flutes with sparkling cider. Even though Hazel was feeling better than usual that day, certain smells still made her nauseated, and alcohol was one of them. Additionally, she'd been advised not to drink during this process, so out of consideration for her the girls had chosen a tamer beverage for the evening.

Callie wasn't complaining. She loved the taste of sparkling cider.

She sipped, taking in the sight of each of her friends. Saffron was in her element, serving drinks and food, which was what she would do all day everyday if she could. They planned to open the restaurant for dinner as well soon, thanks to the influx of Lodge reservations, and Saffron was on top of her professional world.

Too bad she refused to consider the one man who was right for her. At the moment, she was dating some guy from the city who wouldn't even visit Rosebud. Saffron had to drive out to him for all of their dates. Callie gave the relationship about three weeks, tops, before Saffron broke it off.

Kenzie was beaming, the way she seemed to always do these days. Bryan was out camping for the evening with a group of guys he'd met after moving to Rosebud. Their counselor had suggested that he find some interests that were all his own, and that seemed to be working well for the two of them. Things were going so well for them that Kenzie had confided to Callie that they were considering adopting. At nearly fifty, they both felt a little too old to start a family, but Kenzie had said she'd finally felt the maternal instinct kick in, and Bryan had been wanting to at least consider children for a few years now. Kenzie had told Callie the situation would have to be just right, but she felt she should at least think about kids, and Callie had agreed. Kenzie and Bryan had so much love to give.

Laurel was busy ignoring the fact that her ex was behind bars. It was relatively easy to do since the man had no role in her life for the time being. He was paying for his crimes and had asked his family not to visit him while he was incarcerated. Laurel had battled with that declaration. She'd told Bennie it wasn't right for him to be all alone, but he'd convinced her that this was best for all of them. According to Bennie, Laurel and her children had suffered enough, and Laurel had had to agree with that. At least on her children's part. To see their father in prison would just be too much. So they kept their communication to infrequent phone calls and emails. Laurel had worried that wouldn't be enough contact for her children, but Laurel's son Tai had pointed out that they'd barely communicated with their father for a while now—at least since the bomb of his financial indiscretions had exploded. And honestly, a while before that as well. Bennie hadn't had the closest of relationships with any of his children.

So for now Laurel did all she could to make sure her ex didn't leave a void in her kids' lives and that her parents were not dealing with any of the fallout of Bennie's actions. Callie worried that with all that she was doing, Laurel was neglecting herself, but Laurel claimed to be content with her life and Callie had to believe her . . . for now. Although she wondered if Riley might be hoping to give her some of the companionship and hope she needed.

Callie's phone buzzed with a text. *Thinking of you,* was all it said. Was it pathetic that she already missed Leo even though she'd seen him the night before? She'd never felt this way. With every guy she'd dated in the past, Callie had loved her space. A date night a couple of times a week was all she'd needed. That was often why guys broke up with her, since she never really let them in. With Leo, it was different. She couldn't get enough of him. But living a town apart came with challenges. It was hard to see one another daily, even when Callie wanted to. Leo said he wanted it, too. But then there were his kids she had yet to meet and his ex who seemed to still be around . . .

No, Callie wasn't going to think about that. Not tonight. So things weren't perfect with Leo. But they were good, and she was fortunate. At the moment that was enough for her.

"To Hazel," Saffron said after the last glass was passed out. "Since she won't let me sing her a song, I'll give her a toast instead."

Saffron lifted her glass, and the other girls followed suit. "To the only woman who would figure out how to juggle two men even while going through chemo," Saffron teased.

"Hear, hear," Kenzie added as the four of them clinked their glasses.

Hazel kept her glass to herself, glaring at her friends. But there was no heat behind it.

"I'm juggling nothing," she said quietly. Wells was in the next room, and Dylan was downstairs playing video games with Chase and Sterling.

"That's a lie," Laurel said into her glass. She was the least likely of them to tease without cause, so there had to be some truth to it. She would know—she had spent more time with Hazel than the rest of them lately.

"They're both my friends," Hazel spouted.

"You keep telling yourself that, sweetie," Saffron said, patting Hazel's hand before emptying her glass.

"There's no man who would want me in this state. Much

less two," Hazel responded softly, rubbing her bald head as her eyes fell to the table they were sitting around.

Hazel had worn a wrap around her head when they'd first arrived, but had taken it off just minutes into the visit, saying it was too hot. Her eyelashes were gone, and she'd been experimenting with drawing on her eyebrows, since they'd fallen out as well. Her body was frail and a bit too thin, and her skin was pale. But even with all of that, Hazel was still one of the most beautiful women Callie had ever seen in her life.

"Hazel," Callie said, waiting until her friend looked at her. "You are gorgeous, as always."

Hazel scoffed.

"Let me finish," Callie said sternly. "But even if you weren't, you have to know that's not what draws people to you. That light inside of you, Haze—it's been bright since day one. We were all like moths to your flame."

Callie looked around to see each of her friends nodding in agreement.

"So you've lost your hair and have a hard time putting on any weight, but that light is going nowhere. Is it any wonder those two men can't help but flock to you?" Callie saw tears in Hazel's eyes. She didn't want to press anymore, so she stopped.

"I always thought I wasn't a very vain person. But when I started losing my hair, I realized my looks were so much of my identity. Was I still Hazel, looking like this?" Hazel's voice cracked.

"The very best Hazel I know," Kenzie said.

"I don't deserve you all," Hazel said, pulling Kenzie and Saffron, who sat beside her, into a hug. Laurel and Callie moved around the table so they could join.

"You deserve the world, Hazel," Saffron said, her voice muffled because her mouth was pressed into Hazel's shoulder.

"And especially the two hot men fighting over you," Callie had to add.

They dissolved into laughter, because at the end of the day, it's what they always did. Cancer, financial ruin, crumbling relationships, and more had tried to drag the girls down, but with friendship, they could endure anything and always find laughter together.

Made in United States
Orlando, FL
08 November 2022

24332939R00100